THE OUTLAW SHERIFF

From the time they could talk, twins Jim and Jack Allen tracked all their food and learned to shoot and hit any target. Ragged, freckle-faced loner Jim becomes a fugitive and, on occasion, a terrifying killer called the "White Wolf"—but Jack loves law, and is soon the most feared sheriff in Wyoming.

Around the town of Basin, ranchers are losing horses to rustlers, and men are being murdered. They call Jack Allen to eliminate the predators, but Jim assumes Jack's identity—and the White Wolf becomes Basin's sheriff. Jack vows to help Jim—but will he let his brother go free so they can catch their prey together?

THE OUTLAW SHERIFF

Hal Dunning

GUNSMOKE

First published in the UK by Isis

This hardback edition 2008
by BBC Audiobooks Ltd
by arrangement with
Golden West Literary Agency

ISBN 978 1 405 68227 5

British Library Cataloguing in Publication Data available.

Printed and bound in Great Britain by
CPI Antony Rowe, Chippenham, Wiltshire

THE OUTLAW SHERIFF

CHAPTER
ONE

An Arrival

"Ma" Jarrick's expression, as she sat at the head of the table glaring across the plate-cluttered oilcloth at her cow-punchers, warned them all that she was the boss. Red-faced, big-bosomed, strong-armed — she was a dominating figure. The four men who faced her shuffled their feet nervously. She glared at them for a moment:

"Andy Harrison, you toothless old reprobate, and you, 'Baldy', you — listen with both ears. If I hears any more talk of ridin' to Big Rock and wipin' out the Tyson gang, you'll both be out of a job!"

"Now, Ma, you listen!" Baldy mopped his hairless head with a big red bandanna handkerchief, then, gathering his courage in both hands, explained: "We knows for a fact that 'Big-nose' Tyson and his gang is the ones who is makin' our Three Star herd shrivel up like a man in the Salines without water —"

"You knows nothin'!" Ma Jarrick interrupted scornfully. "If you does, why don't you go to Pete Waters and have the moppin' up done regular by the sheriff?"

"Pete Waters!" Ma's son, 'Toothpick', scoffed. "He won't do nothin'. 'Cause why? The bank won't lend you money to pay off the mortgage unless this rustlin' is stopped. And if they don't lend you the money, ain't Pete goin' to foreclose and get the Three Star for a song?"

Toothpick was a tall, wiry youth of nineteen, with curling brown hair and laughing blue eyes, and he usually had his way. But this time he had spoken too impulsively.

"Shut up!" His mother glared at him, and he subsided behind Baldy Jones. "I believe in the law and I won't allow nothin' contrary to it."

Andy Harrison, foreman of the Three Star, a shrivelled, ancient ex-gunman and now a reformed character, was afraid of nothing that wore hair or walked on two feet excepting a woman. But he distrusted the law as only a man can who has been one jump ahead of it for many long years. So Ma's praise of it stirred him from his habitual reticence. Switching his chew to the other side of his toothless mouth and hitching up his gun belt, he mumbled:

"Law is well enough for women, but I calculates to let 'Old Faithful' be my law until I dies. And I says to hell with Pete Waters! He's some sheriff. He goes roaring aroun' like a grizzly, and he ain't got the guts of a rabbit. This business ain't nothin' for a woman to mix in, but, as you says, Mis' Jarrick, you're the boss. So I says, if you want to give over the Three Star to Pete and your cattle to Big-nose, you go to it!"

"You — you —" At a loss for words at Andy's presumption in daring to give her "back talk", Ma Jarrick could only stare. Losing his courage, the old gunman turned and stumped from the room.

"Now, then, if you others has finished fillin' yourselves, get down to the stables and start mendin' harness."

"Skinny" Hicks, a slab-sided, gangling youth of twenty-three, hastily scrambled to his feet and, followed by Baldy Jones and Toothpick, clumped from the room.

The moment Ma Jarrick was alone her expression changed, and she shook her head. For she had as little respect for the law as represented by Pete Waters, the sheriff, as had Andy Harrison.

"The poor lunatics, to go talkin' about wipin' out Tyson's gang. Big-nose would eat all four. And Andy so crippled up by rheumatism that he can hardly ride, much less throw a gun, and them other three that ain't never had a gun fight. Land sakes! Was there such idjuts? They're sure nice boys — aimin' to commit suicide for me — 'cause they knows Big-nose and that there killer, 'Silent Hank', would sure enough massacre 'em! And that boy of mine what thinks he's a man 'cause he packs a gun and is dubbed Toothpick, will be gettin' hisself killed unless I mother him some!"

Tears dimmed her eyes and her face worked convulsively for a moment. Then, to restore her courage, she began to clear the table, rattling the dishes much as a small boy whistles to keep up his nerve.

The home ranch of the Three Star was built where the Roaring River formed a great horseshoe. The

3

cottonwoods and red willows that grew densely along the sheer banks formed a natural windbreak from the icy blasts that swept down from the snow-covered mountain peaks in winter. The dried, rolling plain stretched endlessly to the southwest. But the eye could detect nothing moving there, for the torrid September sun had driven all animal life to cover. Sleep reigned over the range, and a deep silence broken only by the hum of insects and the chirp of birds.

"Gosh darn the thing!" a sleepy voice drawled from the open door of the bunk house. Then becoming louder, ejaculated: "Hey, you fellows is supposed to sew leather — not sleep!"

Andy Harrison glanced at his dozing companions. He made a feeble effort to withdraw the needle from the leather chaps he was stitching, again swore at his companions — then his head nodded, fell back against the door jamb, and he was asleep.

From out of a deep arroyo, a quarter of a mile to the north, two lean, dust-covered grey horses appeared. One carried a small pack and the other the limp form of a man. For a time the horses zig-zagged back and forth like a ship without a rudder; then, striking the home trail, they started along it at a brisk fox-trot.

Ten minutes later Andy Harrison opened his eyes. Staring with wide-open mouth for a moment, with a fervent, muttered oath he vanished in the bunk house. A second later he reappeared with Baldy Jones and pointed to where the two greys were quenching their thirst at the water trough.

"You sure it's him?" Baldy questioned.

"As sure as I'm me," Andy said with conviction. "I've seen him work — et with him a hundred times. Yes, sir, it's him — or his ghost!"

"He looks sort of limplike — all used up. Gosh amighty! He's tied in that saddle!"

The two stared with round eyes at each other for a moment. Then Andy shouted:

"Hey, Jim! *Hey, Jim!*"

"Maybe it's his ghost!" Baldy cried.

At a shambling run, the two started towards the greys. But when they neared them, they slowed to the cautious walk with which one approaches a grizzly not quite dead.

The man on the grey had slumped forward until his head rested on the horse's neck. The only thing that kept him from falling was the two straps that bound him to the saddle.

The two cow-punchers stared at the blood-stained face and head of the rider. Baldy whispered:

"He's dead."

Andy nodded.

"It don't seem possible that 'Jim-twin' Allen was got. There's a lot of folks will sure sleep easier when they hear the little cuss is dead."

"So the 'Killer Wolf' gets killed at last," Baldy remarked sententiously.

Then, as if in denial of these words, the rider swayed, straightened, and muttered:

"Get on, Queen — we're goin' home. One, two, three — one, two, three — one, two, three!"

The muttering of the wounded man galvanised the two cow-punchers into action.

"Quick!" Baldy shrilled, with a new authority born of a terrible excitement. "Loosen them straps and get him under cover."

Carefully lifting him from the saddle, they tenderly carried him to the house. And, as they went, the lean grey horses trotted behind, sniffing like dogs at their master's body.

"Here's a kid that's all shot to pieces," Andy explained gruffly to Ma Jarrick. She had lived too long on the frontier to ask useless questions; so, without a word, she bustled away to prepare the bed in her guest room.

A few minutes later, when Andy stripped off the shirt of the injured man to better dress the jagged wound in the left shoulder, she took one look at the man's torso and gazed at her foreman in awe. For the chest, arms and shoulders were pitted with the scars of former wounds — the livid slashes of knives as well as the puncture marks of bullets.

"Land sakes!" she whispered. "He's been shot to bits heaps of times before this." Then she added irrelevantly: "And he's so small."

There were two fresh wounds — a long, jagged one in the scalp and another in the shoulder. Andy, after a careful examination, dressed them and then looked up at Ma and Baldy.

"It'll take more than them to kill the little cuss. They ain't nothin' but scratches compared to others he's had."

With a grin, he pointed to the scarred chest. Then he continued:

"But he's sure weak from loss of blood."

Later, when they were unsaddling the greys, Baldy rubbed the saddle marks with an expert hand and remarked:

"That saddle ain't been off in two days. Them hosses has been ridden hard. I'm bettin' the fracas he was in happened a long ways up north."

Andy nodded. Then, turning to Skinny Hicks, who, with Toothpick, was watching them curiously, said sharply:

"You take them greys and rub 'em down good. Then throw them in the old corral down in Sunk Meadow."

Something in the way the old gunman gave the order caused Skinny to turn abruptly and hasten to obey without delaying to ask the questions that would appease his curiosity.

"Huh!" Toothpick exclaimed. "What's the row and why-for the blood on them hosses' flanks?"

"Sonny, you remember this — if you ever mention you seen or heard of them two greys, you'll — you'll —" Andy hesitated, then went on soberly: "Toothpick, I wants you to hot-foot it to town and get Doc Spark. If he ain't to be had, don't go bringin' back the sheriff's brother. 'Cause it would be sure better to have no doctor at all than him. And, kid — I knows you can do it — when you're in town don't talk — but listen a lot!"

He gave the young cow-puncher a searching glance. Satisfied with what he found in Toothpick's honest face,

7

he turned and entered the house. Toothpick grinned at Baldy and hurried towards the corral to saddle his horse.

All night long Andy and Ma Jarrick watched by the bedside of the wounded man. Towards midnight the old gunman dozed off, to be aroused later by the shrill voice of their patient. At first he did not know what had awakened him and muttered:

"What is it?"

Ma had her hands pressed tightly over her ears and did not answer but, as Andy turned once more towards the bed, the sick man began to count.

"One, two, three —"

Then he laughed. Even Andy had never heard laughter just like that before. It bit into his ears. Its quality was madness. It had death rather than joy. Once more the man counted — then fell silent.

"He's laughing in hell," Ma cried hysterically.

Andy nodded.

"It ain't natural," Ma said, as she looked down at the thin, boyish, freckled face of the wounded man. "He's too young to feel like that."

"Young?" Then the old gunman added softly: "No, Ma, he's older'n me."

Puzzled, Ma glanced at Andy; it was on her lips to ask what he meant. Then, as she looked again at the wounded man, she caught something — an indefinable something — in that freckled face that brought a sob to her throat and an understanding of Andy's words.

A homely face, with a pug nose covered with freckles so big and brown that even the heavy tan failed to hide them. A big, loose, yet sensitive mouth. The large round eyes, with a curious slant at the corners like those of a wolf, were wide open, unseeing, staring.

If the mouth had been smiling, or the eyes laughing, his age might have been seventeen or eighteen. But, as he lay there, Ma realized that there was something, an intangible something, that gave to him an air of infinite age.

The man began to count again and to mutter flatly, monotonously:

"One, two, three! You're a wolf, so you got to travel alone — so howl, damn you, howl. I'm going; I know I ain't fit for decent folks. One, two, three — go for your gun, 'Red'. Red Dugan, you're goin' to hell at three. One, two three! Howl, damn you, howl! No, you play the game till you cashes in natural —"

"He's so small!" the woman cried irrelevantly. Then, kneeling beside the bed, she raised the man's head against her broad, capable bosom and commenced to sway back and forth like a mother with a child.

"There, there, honey," she crooned. And, as if by magic, her tender words acted like a sedative, the wounded man's muttering grew still, and he slept as peacefully as a child.

Dawn came and turned the eastern sky ablaze. The two still sat there watching.

"Will he live?" the woman asked.

Andy picked his words and answered solemnly:

"Ma, if you loves your boy, if you loves your home — get down on your knees and pray that little cuss, the 'White Wolf', don't cash his chips today!"

CHAPTER
TWO

The Challenge

Big Rock had once aspired to be a metropolis but when the railroad unkindly skipped the town by some two hundred miles, its five hundred inhabitants rapidly shrank to two hundred. Like an inverted T, the town sprawled across the sluggish, muddy creek. Half the ramshackle houses were untenanted and rapidly rotting away. Over all lay the unkempt atmosphere of decay.

It was close to eleven o'clock before Toothpick reached Big Rock and rode down the street towards the Solid Comfort Hotel. He knew his best chance of finding Doctor Spark was there. Later, he would visit the Golden Bar, Big-nose Tyson's drinking palace, and see if he could solve the riddle of those two grey horses and their wounded rider by keeping his ears open.

In the bar-room of the Solid Comfort Hotel, three Bridle Bit cow-punchers clung affectionately to the bar and discoursed with Mike Casey, the owner. One of them, "Tex" Johnson, a tall, thin, sandy-haired cowboy, espied Toothpick and called out:

"Hey! Kid! Lesh have a drink?"

Toothpick grinned and went up to the bar beside them. With the skill that comes of long practice, Mike

10

slid a bottle and four glasses along the sloppy bar towards the three cow-punchers and the newcomer.

The four glasses were filled and emptied. Then Tex leaned towards Toothpick, with that curious, confidential manner of those who have had a drink too many, and said:

"We-all's waitin' for Jim-twin Allen to ride to town."

In a flash the answer to the riddle of those two grey horses came to Toothpick.

"The Wolf sent word he's comin'?" he asked indifferently.

"Not exactly, but —"

"He had a ruckus up north," one of the other cow-punchers interrupted Tex, "and he's headin' this way."

"Big-nose is sure thinkin' of huntin' his hole," the third confided.

"For why?" Toothpick asked.

"'Cause why?" Tex explained. "'Cause The Wolf gunned him once down in the Nations and botched the job and Big-nose figures he's aimin' to make the job complete this time."

"The sheriff says if Jim-twin Allen comes ridin' to town, he'll tie him to his horse's tail and drag —"

Here Mike interrupted. Lowering his voice so it would not carry to the five men playing poker at the other side of the sawdust-covered floor, he said warningly:

"You gents is talkin' loud!"

Tex stared pugnaciously at the burly Mike and scoffed:

"You figure we all are scared of Big-nose and Pete Waters? I'm tellin' you — not any!"

Just the same, from then on Tex and the others carefully avoided using names.

After another drink Toothpick left word with Mike that he wanted to see Doctor Spark, and ducking out of the bar, headed across the street to the Golden Bar.

He found the place jammed with the riff-raff of the town. Here, also, there was talk of Jim-twin Allen. Toothpick slid up to the bar next to two dirty, ill-smelling, typical frontier loafers. Dressed in dirty buckskins, the two made a precarious living as guides to unfortunate tenderfeet. In sentences sprinkled with oaths, they loudly proclaimed what they would do to the "Lobo Wolf" if he dared come to Big Rock.

Seated at a card table, surrounded by his friends, sat Big-nose Tyson, a huge, flabby man whose besotted face told of unrestrained desires. His eyes protruded like two marbles. They were as cold and inexpressive as those of a fish. Big-nose looked soft, yet beneath that soft flesh there lay muscles of steel; while he looked lazy, he possessed the quickness of a snake.

Big-nose caught Toothpick's eye and, grinning evilly, displayed broken yellow teeth. He lifted himself slowly to his feet and lumbered up to the young cow-puncher. As he came, Toothpick marked the ivory-hilted guns that clung closely to either thigh.

Toothpick had all the nerve that goes with youth, but in spite of this he had an almost irresistible temptation to turn and run before the menace in the evil face of the killer.

But after that first impulse to fly had been mastered the younger man waited coolly enough. His greeting to Big-nose was carefully indifferent.

Big-nose unceremoniously pushed the two buckskin-clad men away, and when they turned on him with a snarl, said contemptuously:

"You two gents go catch a coyote before you talk about catchin' a wolf. If Jim-twin Allen came in here you'd both die from runnin'."

With that Big-nose turned an indifferent eye on them and, nodding to the bartender, ordered two drinks. The two guides flushed, and ignoring the amused grins on the faces of the bystanders, slunk away to a safer part of the bar.

"Toothpick," Big-nose said with a touch of sarcasm, "I got a buyer for the Three Star."

"So far as I know, 'tain't for sale." Toothpick tried to make his voice sound indifferent.

"Anyhow, tell your Ma this fellow will give her two thousand more than the mortgage held by Pete Waters."

Toothpick shrugged his shoulders.

" 'Tain't goin' to do her no good to be foolish. If she don't sell, Pete will take it, and two thousand is better than nothin'."

"That mortgage . . ." Toothpick grinned confidentially. "Huh, she reckons to fix that."

From the corner of his eye he saw that several men were listening with interest, and a taunt born of the recklessness of youth sprang to his lips:

"Folks is tellin' me the Lobo Wolf is a-headin' this way."

"Meanin'?" Big-nose said softly, yet with a deadly menace.

"Nothin'!" Toothpick replied easily.

"If The Wolf comes, I ain't aimin' to run, but I'm frank to say I ain't huntin' trouble with him."

Toothpick knew this was the truth. Fear was a sensation unknown to Big-nose. He possessed the cold, savage fury and courage of a black panther. The younger man knew he had but to remain silent and his first remark would be forgotten; but, having the untried courage of youth that finds it necessary to prove itself, he said:

"Yes, Ma was sayin' she reckons to fix that mortgage. The bank is goin' to give her the money." He paused, then went on distinctly: "'Cause we aim to stop the rustlin'!"

The cool audacity of this remark took Big-nose as well as the bystanders by surprise. For everyone there knew, or at least suspected, that the Tyson gang were responsible for the raids on the Three Star cattle. They held their breaths and silently slipped out of range.

For one long moment the bright blue eyes of the younger man gazed into the marble ones of the elder. Then the latter asked softly:

"How does you aim to stop the rustlin'?"

The answer came instantly and without hesitation:

"By catchin' the rustlers. We got a line on 'em!"

"And who be they?" a harsh voice demanded.

Toothpick turned to face this new menace. Silent Hank was Big-nose's lieutenant, and in some ways was far more dangerous than his boss. For, when drunk, he

14

would kill for no other reason than the sheer joy of killing. He was a pockmarked, stoop-shouldered man of fifty. Cruel and unscrupulous, he had the savage instincts of the tiger. The bloodshot eyes were aflame with the lust to fight and kill as he again snarled:

"And who be these rustlers?"

Toothpick was faced by two alternatives. He could lie and say he suspected no one there or he could tell the truth and go for his gun and die. It was Big-nose who saved him from the necessity of making a decision by saying sharply to Silent Hank:

"Not yet!" Then, taking Hank's arm, he led him away and whispered, "If you kill the kid, how will we get the ranch? But if we send word we aim to kill him the next time he comes to town, I reckon his Ma will sell out pronto just to get her kid out of the State safe."

A lonely figure, Toothpick stood at the end of the bar for a few minutes; then he strolled outside. The fact that no one had joined him after Big-nose left, told him plainly that he was a marked man, and that no one there wished to take a chance.

He was only an untried boy who had faced a difficult situation bravely enough, but, once outside, the reaction set in, and he was forced to lean against a tree for several moments to regain his composure.

A little later he found Doctor Spark, and the two started on the return journey to the Three Star Ranch. While Toothpick was waiting for the doctor to saddle his horse, he seized the opportunity to read the account in the county-seat newspaper of a double killing in Olmstead Ville, a town two hundred miles to the north.

The article was headed: "Jim-twin Allen Rides to Town."

And, as the two rode through the silent night, Toothpick found it strangely consoling that the hero of that story was lying wounded at the Three Star Ranch.

The road from Big Rock to the Three Star lay along the bed of an ancient river. This was perhaps a mile wide, smooth-floored and hemmed in by sheer bluffs a hundred feet high.

Toothpick and the doctor made good time on the return to the ranch. They rode mostly in silence. The horses, as they single-footed along the fine white sand of the roadway, made not a sound. The stillness of the night was broken only by the hoot of an owl, or the scream of a distant mountain lion.

In such a setting, it was only natural that Toothpick's mind should be active and his imagination keen. He wondered about the wounded man, who, he was now certain, was the outlaw, Jim-twin Allen. Toothpick knew there was sufficient reward for Allen, dead or alive, to pay the mortgage twice over; yet, it can be said to his credit, never once did he consider turning the outlaw over to the law.

He recalled the conflicting stories he had heard about Jim-twin Allen — conflicting in all ways excepting in regard to his ferocious and reckless bravery. By some he was held to be the worst murderer ever known in the West — one who was driven to kill by a blood lust. Others considered him a blessing to the country and said: "He never killed none who didn't need killing." Some said he was the fabled Lone Wolf —

16

outlawed by his pack — condemned to travel ever alone because his kind feared and could not trust him; others swore he was the White Wolf of Indian fable, who brought good luck, and that none but the evil need fear him!

Then, as if reading the boy's thoughts, the doctor turned in his saddle and said:

"Is The Wolf bad hurt?"

Shocked, surprised that the doctor should have guessed the identity of the wounded man, Toothpick stammered:

"The Wolf?"

"Yeh," the doctor said dryly. "I read the account in the newspaper of the rumpus up north, and it ain't possible Allen could have escaped scot-free."

Toothpick thought of just what this might portend and replied:

"He's sure bad hurt. He rode two hundred miles shot to bits."

"With twenty men ridin' at his heels!" the doctor added gravely. Then, noting the expression on Toothpick's face, said:

"Don't you worry none, sonny. The reward on Allen would sure do a heap of things for me except make me happy. Any man with guts enough to walk into Red's place up north, and then start countin' his damn 'One, two, three' to give Red a chance, is safe from me even if there was a million reward for him!"

"The paper says there was a dozen men takin' pot shots at him before he could get out after he downed Red and 'Silver Tip'. "

They fell again into silence.

When the two arrived at the Three Star, Allen was conscious. He lay quiet and still while the doctor probed for the bullet in his shoulder and cleaned and dressed the wound on his head. He was like a man dead, incapable of feeling, and his ageless expression never altered.

A little later Toothpick quieted old Andy's fears by telling him the doctor knew Allen's identity and there was no danger of his talking. Then he related his passage with Big-nose and listened meekly to the old gunman's scolding.

"You dang fool!" Andy stormed. "Ain't you got no sense nohow? I'm tellin' you even when I was young, and experts thought me fast, I'd have given that hombre a wide berth. He's hell on wheels and would even make The Wolf hustle to beat him to it. And I'm tellin' you Big-nose is so good that if Jim Allen walked in and started countin' like he did with Red up north, Big-nose would drop him. So what chance you got? None whatsoever. Now you stay away from town and let that killer cool down!"

Toothpick knew this was sense, knew he had acted the part of a foolish, hot-headed boy, but — he intended some day to ride back to town.

After partaking of breakfast, the doctor went back to Big Rock, and the Three Star settled down to the grinding work of rounding up and cutting out one hundred two-year-olds. It was on these that Ma was depending to pay off the mortgage.

It was three days later that "Scarface" arrived with Big-nose's ultimatum. He was a short, blowsy, truculent individual of mixed blood. He had inherited all the vices of an Irish father and Apache mother. But none of their virtues.

His air was insolent as he lolled in the saddle and leered down at the Three Star punchers. It was noon. They had just finished dinner and were saddling in the corral when he rode up.

"Toothpick," Scarface said, "Big-nose tole me to tell you the next time you come to town you will utter in public that you weren't meanin' him when you done so much talkin' about rustlers, or you will go for your gun — and get planted!"

The boy looked up at him coolly; then switching the tooth-pick, from which he had derived his nickname, to the other side of his mouth, drawled:

"You can tell Big-nose when I come to Big Rock I'll say my say."

"And you've got ten seconds to hit the breeze, or you'll swallow dust!" Andy snarled, with one rheumatic hand twitching close to his gun butt.

"Sure! There's four of ye," Scarface sneered as he swung his pony about. "But you'll talk soft and pretty if I catch you alone in town."

Furious, Andy again let loose his wrath on Toothpick and cursed him for a fool. The younger man listened in silence. Then, when Andy had finished his tirade, said quietly:

"What's done is done. You ain't askin' me to stay away from town or run for it, is you?"

"Not any," Andy replied miserably. Then warned: "But don't go hurrying things!"

19

CHAPTER
THREE

Stolen Pie

Four days later Allen had sufficiently recovered to totter out to the dining room and take dinner with the others. He was a comical little figure with his freckled face peering from the bandages that encircled his head. And his constant chatter kept the men in a continual state of mirth. For he had a way of relating stories of things that had happened to him as if the joke were always on him.

A week after he had ridden into the ranch he was strong enough to totter down to the old pasture to see his pets. He insisted on going alone. He was shy of witnesses to his meeting with the beasts whom he trusted above men — with the only living things in whom he had complete confidence.

The following night Skinny was shot. Ma Jarrick had gathered the hundred two-year-olds and was holding them in a box canyon for a buyer who was to arrive at the end of the week. Skinny was standing night guard when he was murdered — cruelly and cold-bloodedly — and the cattle had been run off.

At daybreak, Baldy had gone to relieve Skinny, and had found him lying on his face in a clump of thorny brush. Gently, Baldy had turned the prone figure over, and, with rage in his heart, had observed the slack jaws and staring, blinded eyes. Hatred for the perpetrators of the wanton deed increased the cow-puncher's speed as he galloped back to the ranch with the news.

Ma was in the kitchen preparing their breakfasts, and Andy decided to keep the news from her until it was certain the cattle could not be traced.

Two passing neighbours were pressed into service, one to ride to Big Rock for the sheriff, and the other to request help from the Bridle Bit Ranch some few miles up the river.

Allen, riding a big buckskin, accompanied Toothpick to the scene of the crime and sat listlessly in the saddle, watching the young cow-puncher searching for signs of the murderers.

Suddenly Toothpick turned and cried:

"Come over here — I got something to show you."

Pointing to some marks on the ground, Toothpick continued:

"This is where them two damned skunks hid when they ambushed him. They didn't give him a chance!"

Jimmy swung himself from the saddle and said:

"They lay there for about an hour waitin' for enough light to line their sights." Then, glancing at the ground, he added:

"One of them was short and the other a tall, skinny fellow."

Toothpick stared, then inwardly told himself that Jim Allen was exaggerating; that he could not see that from the evidence there was. But a little later, after Jim had unerringly led the way to where there were signs of two

21

horses having been picketed, Toothpick was willing to admit Allen could see things hidden from him.

Toothpick grinned at Allen's antics as he beat about among the bushes like a setter dog hunting for a wounded bird. It seemed to him as if the other's nose was working as well as his eyes.

"The tall gent rode a sorrel with two nails missin' from the hind off-shoe. The short gent straddled a black."

Toothpick showed his unbelief at this, and Jim hastened to point out horsehair clinging on the bushes, as well as certain prints.

"You got me beat," Toothpick cried in amazement. "You can sure follow a trail."

"When I was a kid, my dad — he used to make a trail to our grub and, if me and my brother couldn't follow, we went hungry. We near starved. Maybe that's what made us so small."

"Didn't know you had a brother," Toothpick exclaimed.

Allen grinned.

"We don't see much of one another now."

"What does he do?"

"He's a sheriff up north."

Toothpick laughed.

"But you sure learned how to follow a trail."

"You bet we did," Jim agreed, hesitated, and went on eagerly:

"I tell you — you go steal a pie, hide it somewhere, and if I don't find it, I'll give you a hundred dollars!"

22

"Nix!" Toothpick chuckled. "If you want pie, go steal it yourself."

He laughed aloud at the comical look of disappointment on Allen's face as he sighed: "I dassen't!"

"What you aimin' to do about Big-nose?" Jim asked as they rode back to the ranch house.

"When I feels like it I'm goin' to town," Toothpick responded simply.

Jim cast a keen glance at the youth; and while he detected worry in the blue eyes, he saw no fear.

"Reckon you would," he said. "Can you throw a gun?"

Toothpick flushed, then replied: "I'm no slouch, but . . ."

They had reached a clump of tall, dense, thorny brush which completely screened them from the view of anyone in the house. The little gunman swung from his saddle and said:

"Let's see you work."

Embarrassed, Toothpick hesitated for a second. Then, with what speed he possessed, snatched out his Colt.

"Don't jerk at it. Let your hand drag it out and up with one movement. Like this!" Jim flashed his hand to his hip and his gun exploded.

"I forgot —" Flushing like a schoolboy, Allen turned an apologetic face to Toothpick. "Don't think I'm bein' smart but — I can't draw the thing without its goin' off."

23

They walked together towards the house and Jim explained:

"You see, the whole thing is one movement with me, and I can't separate them."

Never for a moment had Toothpick suspected Allen of trying to show off. His only emotion had been one of shock, for he had not seen Jim-twin Allen's hand move.

This made him thoughtful, for it proved how much he had to learn, and brought home to him a sickening conviction that his chances in the coming encounter with Big-nose were not worth figuring.

"Now then, you jaspers!" Ma cried angrily at dinner that day. "Which one of you stole my pie?"

"Pie?" mumbled Jim. "A pie is stole?"

"Yes, stole," she snapped. "And me bakin' my head off feedin' you galoots — and you has to steal as if I didn't feed you right."

With that she was off to the kitchen and slammed the door behind her. It was Ma's custom, when under great stress of mind, to walk along the path that followed the winding river. Through the thinning bushes, she saw a sight on the opposite bank that brought her to an amazed halt.

"Lands sake!" she cried. "I never did see a sight like that before."

Directly opposite, scarcely twenty yards away, was Jim-twin Allen. He was seated on the ground with his back to a rock, and on his lap was a large pie.

But it was not the fact that she had caught the pie thief that astonished her; but that he was feeding the pie to the two grey horses.

Prancing, squealing, their vicious eyes agleam, their teeth bared, they were snapping at each other and at their laughing master.

"Now, then, you —"

Even Ma, with her vast experience, was dumbfounded and a little appalled at the string of oaths that sprang from the man's lips. Yet she realized each oath was an endearment.

"You, Queen — Princess — you two useless bags of bones — stand!"

The last word snapped out like the crack of a whip and instantly the horses became still.

"You, Queen, you're first — 'cause you're oldest."

One horse stretched up its neck and snapped up the offered pie. The other gave a squeal and lashed out with its hind legs for being kept waiting.

First one then the other was fed. Then he would take a bite himself. At last the plate was empty.

"I tell you it's all gone!" he cried as the horses recommenced their squealing and snapping. To Ma, their teeth sounded like the rattle of castanets.

Allen, ignoring the two beasts, who trotted along behind, nipping his shoulders, walked rapidly towards the house.

Little by little Ma's amazement and slight anger disappeared and gave place to pity and understanding that a man's loneliness should force him to make companions of two horses.

Later she confronted Jim and pointed an accusing finger at the crumbs on his shirt.

He looked guiltily at her and stammered:

"I'm caught and I'm awful sorry, but you see, ma'am —"

"Ma," she corrected.

"Ma, then," he answered, with one of his likeable grins.

"You been feedin' my pie to them ugly brutes of yours," she accused.

"Them hosses; Ma, they ain't brutes — they're humans!" he cried in quick defence.

"Why didn't you ask me for it, 'stead of stealin' it?" she demanded.

"I knows how hard it is to make good pie, and I figured you'd be peeved and think I was wasting it, if you ketched me feedin' it to them, but them old bags of bones ain't hosses. They is humans and knows more about pie than most folks!"

There was something so pathetic in the earnestness with which he spoke of his pets that Ma suddenly reached forward and drew him to her ample bosom.

"You poor boy," she said as she patted his shoulder and smoothed his rumpled hair. "Imagine havin' to make friends with a dumb brute!"

A second later he broke away. His face was flaming with embarrassment as he stammered:

"You oughtn't to do that, 'cause, you see, I — my hands — I ain't fit to be touched!"

With that he turned and scuttled through the door. Outside he confided to Toothpick:

26

"Women is terrible! They sure make you feel silly and wormlike."

Toothpick turned and studied the far-distant peaks for a moment. It is sometimes best not to see a man when he has tears in his eyes. Especially when that man has the reputation of Jim-twin Allen.

Ma had been told of the death of Skinny and of the theft of her cattle. That night supper was eaten in abysmal gloom, for Skinny had been a favourite with all. But there was not only this — there was also the fact that the hundred two-year-olds Ma had figured on to save the ranch were gone forever.

That afternoon had been spent by Andy and several neighbours in a desperate attempt to track the cattle, but the trail had been lost in a maze of blind arroyos in the Bad Lands. This was a final blow and all there knew that, excepting for a miracle, the Three Star was lost. In another week it would be the property of Pete Waters, the sheriff.

News arrived late that evening that Pete Waters and his brother, the coroner, were due at the ranch the following morning to investigate the killing of Skinny. No one there expected that Ma's last appeal to Pete's better nature would be effective.

Yet, in spite of their forebodings, the men ate heartily. That is, with the exception of Allen, who scarcely touched his food and seldom removed his eyes from the plate before him during the whole meal.

The moment their plates were clean, Andy and Toothpick pushed back their chairs and clattered off to the bunk house.

27

After they had left, Jimmy picked up his hat, turned to Ma and said:

"Ma'am." He hesitated over his next words. "I'm thankin' you a lot and askin' you to forgive me for stealin' your pie — and — and other things."

Ma could never understand just why or what it was about Jim that made her want to cry. Even when he was grinning and joking with the others, she felt his laughter was not real. She had once confided to Andy:

"He laughs with his big mouth, but not with his eyes."

So now, as he stood before her with his eyes on the floor, a lump came into her throat and she said huskily:

"What ails you? Pie — that wasn't nothin' at all."

"That ain't all," he continued miserably. "I've been foolin' you. Never mind — you'll learn some day. Just remember I'm thankin' you a lot."

"You're leavin'?" she queried in surprise.

"Yes, Ma; before sunup — I got lots to do tomorrow."

"Tush and nonsense! You ain't strong enough to go cavortin' about."

"I reckon it's best for me to kinda slide out inconspicuous before the sheriff comes tomorrow."

"Oh!" She remembered his scarred body and partially understood. "But you can come back later and get some more pie."

"I won't be stayin' long — but maybe I'll just be stoppin' to say, 'Hello', so it would be right nice of you to have a pie wrapped up for me to take along."

"Two pies," she corrected, and was amused by the greedy look that came into his face at the mention of anything sweet. "One for you and one for the greys."

He nodded and, before she could say more, slipped through the door and was gone.

"I don't care what he's done. I just know he never done nothin' wrong," she cried as she turned to enter her bedroom.

Jimmy did not sleep in the bunk house, but spent the night, curled up like a dog, beneath a clump of thorny brush.

"Those hombres — if they're aimin' to scare Ma into sellin' out — which I figure they is — might return to other devilment. So we'll kinda keep watch tonight, then go talk to 'em tomorrow!"

Nothing happened to disturb his watch, and at the first grey streak of dawn he saddled one of the greys and headed for the Bad Lands.

CHAPTER
FOUR

Mary Ann

About two hours after sunup, Pete Waters and his brother, the coroner, arrived. The sheriff was a powerfully built man of forty. He had a deep, booming, bass voice and this, with his air of ponderous dignity, was his chief political asset. At heart he was far too cowardly to be really bad, and clung to his office because he knew a man had to be utterly reckless before he would turn a gun on a sheriff. Among most people he had a reputation for courage, but the more discriminating keenly suspected he had a yellow streak a yard wide.

It fell to Toothpick to show the sheriff and coroner the body and to point out later the various things Allen had shown him on the day before.

In a heavy silence, the sheriff listened to Toothpick's explanation as to why he thought one of the murderers was short and the other tall.

Then, with a derogatory gesture of his hands, he dismissed the evidence.

"Kid, you're romancin'. Don't try to show off. If there was anything to prove you right, I'd listen. But

I've had a lot more experience than you, and if I can't see them things, I reckon you can't neither."

When they returned to the house Ma made one last appeal for more time in which to pay the mortgage. But the sheriff shook his head.

"Mis' Jarrick," he said hypocritically, "I'm plumb sorry. If you was a man, now, and could run things out here, I'd give you all the time you wanted. But you is a woman and you're sure to lose."

"Then why don't you help me catch the rustlers?"

"Now, ma'am, don't be unreasonable," he responded in the manner of one reproving a child. "This ain't the only ranch. I've got a dozen to watch out for, and folks is expected to do their part in helpin' me."

"Ma! *Ma!*" Baldy cried hysterically as he bounced into the room. "Come quick!"

With her heart in her mouth, for fear of some new calamity, Ma followed him outside.

Baldy was almost beside himself with excitement. He waved an excited arm towards the Bad Lands. Ma looked and gasped in bewilderment.

For there, coming up the swale from the Bad Lands were her lost cattle. Bawling and surrounded by a cloud of dust, they were rushing towards her as if trying to escape from the devil.

"They're comin' home by themselves," Baldy cried in wonder.

But Ma knew this was untrue for she saw two grey streaks, and mounted on one of them was a diminutive figure she knew.

The sheriff, after the first excitement had died down, did what he could to hide his disappointment and congratulated her on the mysterious return of her cattle.

"Now, then," cried Ma, "as soon as I sell them, I'll pay you the money."

The mysterious return of the cattle was a seven-day wonder among the Three Star outfit. And on the following day, when two riderless horses found their way back to Big Rock, people did much speculating as to what had happened to their riders, "Nigger" Jones and "Red" Mike.

What happened to them was never known, for they vanished completely and were never seen again. And the manner of their taking off will forever remain a mystery.

A little after noon that day a small man, riding a big buckskin with the Three Star brand on its flank, rode down the dust-littered main street of Big Rock. He was dressed in a tattered pair of overalls much too large for him. He wore no guns that could be seen, and the bandages on his head had been so arranged as almost completely to hide his face.

A loafer, seated before Hick's livery stable, glanced listlessly at him and decided he was some kid from a distant ranch.

Allen swung from his horse before the Comfort Hotel and dropping the reins over the hitch rail, stood for a moment gazing about like a gawky country boy on his first trip to town.

He wandered aimlessly along the street. Then, spying some bright-coloured candy bars in the general-store window, ducked in for a moment and reappeared with his mouth filled with the sticky mess. Sucking hard at a stick of candy, he slipped through the swinging doors of the Golden Bar. He marked the position of the bar, the windows, and the tables; then wandered again outside.

"We won't be eatin' candy the next time we pays a visit to that there drinkin' palace," he confided to his horse as he swung into the saddle.

Riding a short distance up the trail, he dismounted and catnapped until the sheriff and coroner returned from the Three Star. Fifteen minutes later he went to the sheriff's house.

When the sheriff had answered the door, and the boy had explained his errand, the officer exclaimed:

"Who are you? I ain't never seed you before. How come Ma trusted you with that money?"

Allen squirmed, then grinned.

"It don't make no difference who I be — I got the money, and money talks — not kids." Then when he saw another question trembling on the sheriff's lips, he hastily added:

"Gosh, mister, I was scared havin' all this money on me with this outlaw, the Killer Wolf, runnin' around."

"Don't you be scared of him!" The sheriff laughed grandly. "He knows enough to keep out of my county. I'll tie him to my horse's tail if he comes, and let you prod him through town for folks to look at."

"Yeh, I bet you could. I bet you're sure strong and could lick a dozen Wolfs, couldn't you?" While this was said in a guileless and sincere manner, there was a certain quality in the voice that made the sheriff look sharply at the boy. Satisfied with what he saw in that freckled face — at least as much as he could see of it — he smiled tolerantly and said:

"Yeh, I reckon I could."

"Ma wants me to pay you today, so she said to please ask you to ride over to the county seat and let me pay you the money before Judge Wilks. And I hope you will, because I want to get shot of this money."

The sheriff considered a moment. He might as well accept payment today. Besides, there were certain things he wished to see about at the county seat.

"All right, sonny, you meet me down the street near the Golden Bar and we'll go over together."

The sheriff nodded and re-entered the house, and the boy started down the street. If the sheriff could have seen the look of unholy glee on his face, his complacency might have been badly shattered. Suddenly Jim's expression altered.

Two ancient prospectors were sitting on a horse block, sunning themselves before Goldburg's General Store. One was a stranger, but the other was "Pop" Jones. Jim knew him well. The moment Jim's eyes fell on them a ready-made plan leaped to his mind. He remembered Pop's locoed mule, which would return to Big Rock and its master no matter how far it had been sent from home.

Slipping noiselessly up, Jimmy, casting a hasty glance behind him, gave the taller, white-whiskered prospector a resounding slap on the back.

With a howl of rage the old man leaped to his feet and thrusting out gnarled hands, attempted to seize and chastise the fresh kid with the bandaged head who had dared disturb his repose.

"Punch the kid's nose, Pop," advised his companion.

The ancient prospector cast one glimpse at Allen. Then his expression changed and he said sheepishly:

"Gosh, Jim, I didn't know you with all that stuff you got on your head. How's your health?"

"Stuffed full of pie," Jim replied with an ingratiating grin.

"Pie? Ha-ha!" the old man roared. "You always was strong for sweets and women's feed."

"Huh, Pop, who's your friend?" the other prospector inquired aggrievedly.

Pop chose to ignore his partner.

The old fellow looked at him disgustedly and reseated himself with his back to the others.

"You still got Mary Ann?" Jim asked.

"You bet. I can't never lose that mule. Sold her three times, but she always comes back. Only way I can get rid of Mary Ann is with an axe," Pop mournfully complained.

"I'm givin' you fifty cash for Mary Ann." Jim grinned at the puzzled expression in Pop's eyes and added: "You know that old shed in the wash just off the Stony Gulch trail?"

Pop nodded.

"You tie Mary Ann there. And see you fix her so she can't get loose nohow."

Again Pop nodded. Jim handed him the money and shook his head in answer to the pleading, curious look in Pop's ancient eyes.

"You old reprobate, you tie that mule so she can't get loose or — or —" Jimmy grinned and added: "She'll be coming back to you later with a present tied to her tail."

Then, catching sight of the sheriff at the farther end of the street, he ran to his horse and swung into the saddle, and hurried to meet the representative of the law.

"What for you let that little runt ride you?" "Grumpy" snorted.

"'Cause he once kept me from bein' cooked by an Apache," Pop grunted.

"Who's he?"

"None of your business," Pop cried cryptically. Then he ambled off to collect Mary Ann and to convey her to the cabin.

Jim and the sheriff made the six miles to the county seat in little less than an hour. Their trip was quite uneventful. Jim talked and nearly drove the sheriff crazy with his constant gabble. The sheriff was in a bad temper to start out with, for he had planned to take over the Three Star Ranch within the next few days, and Allen's proposed payment of the mortgage ruined all his carefully laid schemes.

At length the harassed man gruffly ordered him to shut his gab. Upon this Allen began to sing, which, if anything, the officer found more trying than the boy's garrulity.

36

It was with positive relief that the sheriff rode down the tin-littered street to the judge's office.

Here things were quickly settled. Jim produced the necessary two thousand dollars, partly in gold and partly in bills. This was paid to the sheriff, the mortgage cancelled, handed to Jim, and a record of the payment entered in the county's books.

After that the three repaired to a nearby saloon before the sheriff went to deposit his money in the bank.

The drinks consumed, the sheriff deposited his money in the bank and then made the unpleasant discovery that the boy intended to return to Big Rock with him.

If Jim had been garrulous on the journey to Willow Creek, he was just the reverse on their return. He seldom opened his mouth. The sheriff became vaguely alarmed. There was something intangible — something that seemed to mock him — in the other's dark eyes. After a moment's thought the sheriff dismissed his fears and began to banter and joke with his young companion.

The two were crossing the creek a short distance from the cabin when Allen laughed aloud as the "he-haw" of a mule reached his ears.

The sheriff turned to inquire the reason for the boy's mirth and stared into the muzzle of a large black Colt.

Caught absolutely by surprise, he stared with fascination into the pistol barrel. His jaw dropped — his florid face became redder — his ridiculous eyes protruded.

"I'm Jim-twin Allen," the man holding the gun advised crisply. At this the blood in the sheriff's face drained away and left it a chalky, ghastly white.

"Loosen your belt and let it drop. Then slide off your hoss gentlelike and keep your hands where I can see 'em!"

Allen's voice had the edge of steel. The big sheriff obeyed his orders implicitly. He turned slowly and thrust his hands behind him. Deftly Jim threw a noose about them and bound them tight.

Pete growled out threats mingled with oaths. But the other, quite unperturbed by the future, calmly finished binding his victim.

Having trussed the sheriff's arms close to his body, much as one binds a goose's wings when preparing it for the oven, Allen fastened a large collar about Pete Waters' neck.

"I figure it's best you do no shoutin'." Jim grinned as he thrust Pete's handkerchief into its owner's mouth.

Then having rendered him silent as well as helpless, Jim-twin Allen prodded him down the path towards Mary Ann.

The mule was tugging at her halter in a desperate effort to free herself. But with the memory of many beatings in her mind, promptly desisted in her efforts the moment the two men approached. She drooped her ears and waited patiently for what was to come.

Allen carefully attached one end of a short rope to the collar on the sheriff's neck and tied the other end to the mule's tail. Mary Ann turned and watched the operation with a red, reproachful eye, but offered no visible objection.

"Now, Mister Sheriff — I'm doin' this for the good of your soul," Allen said as he finished tying the rope to the tuft on the mule's tail. "And just you think twice afore you go houndin' helpless widows again. 'Cause the next time — after the next time there won't be no next time."

He gave a shrill whistle, and the two greys came galloping up from a gully a short distance away. He stripped the bandages from his head and then, taking two belts and holsters from the pack on one of the greys, fastened the belts on, thrust the guns into the holsters and carefully tied them to his legs. Then turning to the sheriff, he added:

"I'm payin' a visit to Big Rock, and I figure folks will be hollerin' out loud for their sheriff pronto, but I'm trustin' Mary Ann to get you there in time. And I'm warnin' you to stay on your feet, 'cause if you stumble and fall — or get stubborn and try and sit — you'll sure commit suicide. For Mary Ann will sure drag you to kingdom come — or Big Rock."

With that Jimmy turned Mary Ann loose. Without waiting to see the success of his scheme, for he had faith in that mule's homing instinct, he swung on one of his greys and headed for Big Rock.

CHAPTER
FIVE

Three Men

Before the sheriff had left the Three Star that forenoon, when he and his brother, the coroner, had been out to investigate the murder of Skinny, he had handed Toothpick a letter. Both he and his brother had been mounted when the sheriff had leaned down and whispered in an undertone to Toothpick:

"Got a note for you." There was a malicious twinkle in his eye as he added: "Good thing I didn't forget it."

Away from his mother's unsuspecting eye, Toothpick ripped open the letter and read:

If u got the guts of a skunk u will come and spout out loud that u never ment I was a rustler or smoak it out with me. I'll be waitin' for u at the Golden Bar at 6p.m. I'm nailin' a copy of this here speshul in the post office.

yours till u die
BIG-NOSE TYSON.

Having finished this short death warrant, Toothpick looked up at the sheriff, and after coolly studying him for a moment, said:

40

"You can tell your friend I'll be there."

The sheriff started to speak, thought better of it, and swung his horse about for the return journey to Big Rock.

Toothpick slowly walked behind the stables and gave a few minutes of earnest practice to the draw Allen had taught him. But at the end of a short time he gave it up and decided to stick to his old method. He did not have time to learn a new one.

Shortly after dinner he saddled his pony, and without telling anyone where he was going, headed for town. Arriving there he entered the Solid Comfort Hotel and had a lonely drink. Mike, the bartender, volunteered the information that the gang were all over at the Golden Bar.

Thus Toothpick realized that the whole town were advised of the coming encounter and were making merry at the other place while waiting to see him die.

He knew that it was only by the rarest good luck that he could hope to emerge a winner from the coming encounter. While internally he was very sober and thoughtful, outwardly he gave no indication of his feelings.

"The kid has nerve," Mike told himself after Toothpick had left the bar and headed for the one across the street.

Toothpick hesitated for a fraction of a second before he pushed open the swinging door of the bar. Once inside he coolly surveyed the inmates, who nervously avoided his glance.

The place was packed. If Big-nose's challenge had done nothing else, it had brought him a roaring business, for a huge crowd jostled and swirled before the bar.

Bets were freely made that Toothpick would not come. Five to one was offered and no takers, that, if he did come, he would go out feet first.

With Toothpick's entrance, the babble sank and then rose again. The bar was crowded. But Toothpick had no difficulty finding a place, for the mob shrank away from him as if he were the plague. He stood in lonely grandeur at one end of the bar.

Nodding to the barman, he ordered whisky, which he twirled in his left hand but did not drink. One minute, five minutes passed. Still Big-nose made no movement towards him. Toothpick had glimpsed Big-nose as he entered. The man was seated at a table in the rear with Silent Hank and Scarface. Toothpick waited impatiently. Then a movement of the crowd told him his enemy was coming towards him.

Like magic the crowd split apart.

"It's a shame," Pop, the old prospector confided to his partner Grumpy. "The kid has nerve, but he ain't got a dog's chance."

As Big-nose started ponderously towards Toothpick, the swinging doors opened and a small figure entered.

Toothpick glimpsed him from the corner of his eye and turned squarely towards him. No longer was Allen the harmless, likeable, freckle-faced kid. Everyone there who saw him, even before their slow wits told them the truth, recognised in him a relentless force of destruction. It was not the two guns worn low down on his thighs, but his face that held their attention.

It was drawn into a thousand little wrinkles; the corners of his lips were drawn up; his eyes were yellow flames. There was something impersonal in his face that made it as terrifying as a calamity of nature — a tornado — a cloudburst.

Walking stiff-legged like a fighting wolf, yellow eyes flaring, body loose and swaying, hands swinging close to his guns, he headed towards the advancing hulk of Big-nose Tyson.

A murmur swept the room.

"Jim-twin Allen!"

"The White Wolf!"

Big-nose was evil, but he was no coward. He would never have deliberately sought a meeting with Jim-twin Allen, but he had the nerve to meet it now it was here. Slowly he turned and edged away from the press of the crowd. He wanted room for his draw.

The crowd melted away as snow melts before the spring sun.

Both Silent Hank and Scarface came slowly to their feet. Toothpick tried to shout a warning to Jim to watch Hank and Scarface, but when he opened his mouth no words came from his parched palate.

A heavy silence!

Silent Hank instantly made his plan of action. He knew Jim was watching him and felt that the first of the three to make a play would be the first to receive Allen's fire. Both he and Scarface were behind and to the right of Big-nose. Silent Hank decided to wait until

43

his boss started to draw before he went into action. He hoped by this plan to get a free shot at Allen.

"Gents, I'm countin' three! One!"

At that Big-nose went for his guns.

The glasses and bottles on the shelves behind the bar leaped about with the heavy concussion. Blue smoke, pierced by red flames, swirled about in rings.

The walls of the low-ceilinged room caught and tossed back echoes of the thunderous reports. As quickly as the uproar had started it hushed.

Big-nose's hands had flashed faster than the eye could follow to the butts of his ivory-handled Colts. But, fast as he was, he was not fast enough. Before his guns came level, destruction smashed him in the stomach. The gun in the right hand exploded and a bullet tore through the floor. Then he staggered, wavered, pitched forward on his face.

As Allen fired he leaped to the left and for the second Big-nose remained on his feet, he offered a shield from the fire of Silent Hank and Scarface.

Both the men's guns were out by the time their boss collapsed. But Allen's jump had upset them for the fraction of a moment; so, when he leaped over the fallen body of Big-nose, it was they and not he who received the first fire.

Neither fired before Allen's bullets got them. Silent Hank drew himself up very straight then, like a falling post, toppled to the floor. Scarface received two slugs simultaneously which tossed him into a corner, where he lay like a crumpled bundle of clothes.

Then silence — complete.

44

The Wolf commenced to laugh — strange laughter that bit into the onlookers' consciousness and left them incapable of action — mocking yet mirthless.

No one stirred as Jim-twin Allen moved backwards towards the door; a moment he stood there and was gone.

Slowly the bystanders recovered their senses. They stared at the three dead men in amazement and mingled awe.

"He got all three!"

It was the bartender who first raised the shout:

"The sheriff — get him! There's a fortune on that little devil's head!"

"Sheriff! Quick, get the sheriff!"

The crowd flowed pell-mell into the street and started at the sight that met their eyes.

Without hurry, deliberately, Mary Ann came down the centre of the street. Behind her, red-faced, furious, maddened with shame, willy-nilly, came the sheriff.

When he saw the crowd he desperately attempted to hold back the mule. She dragged him forward — up to them and by them. When they saw the placard about Mary Ann's neck their tension of the moment before disappeared, and they roared with insane laughter. They howled their mirth and slapped each other on the back as they remembered Pete Waters' boast. The placard read:

RETURNED WITH THANKS —

Jim-twin Allen.

★ ★ ★

Above a distant mountain peak on the far horizon arose the full moon. It gilded a few lazy, drifting clouds with its wan gold, and distilled the prairie's black shadows to purple.

Before the darkened doorway of the Three Star Ranch stood the lonely figure of a woman. Ma was awaiting the messenger who would bring her news of the death of her son. She had guessed the mission of Toothpick when she first discovered his absence.

But the messenger of death never came. Allen was riding one grey and was followed by the other when he trotted up to her and asked cheerfully:

"You got them pies?" In answer to the question in her eyes he laughed and said: "Toothpick's all right."

For a moment joy rendered her incapable of speech. "Thank God!"

Pointing back the way he had come, he explained:

"Ma, I can't wait, but here's a present for you. You don't owe me nothin'. You get the pies and then I'll give it to you."

Ma vanished and then reappeared with a bundle. Grinning, Allen handed her the envelope containing the cancelled mortgage and then rode off to the west.

A moment later, while she still clutched it to her plump bosom, he vanished in the darkness. But Ma, unknowing what he had done for her that day, wept that he should be going, and waited until the clatter of his horses' hoofs had died away in the distance.

CHAPTER
SIX

A Horse Deal

The little town of Beaverville sprawled along the banks of Muddy Creek. Its streets, cluttered with broken bottles, old tin cans, and bits of harness, were knee-deep in dust.

In the bar-room of the Lone Star Hotel, three dusty cow-punchers clung affectionately to the bar while they discoursed with Mike Horigan, the owner. One of the three, Toothpick Jarrick, steadied himself, leaned across the bar and whispered confidentially:

"Lesh 'ave 'nother." Grinning brightly, he added: "'Ave one yershelf, Mike."

Skilfully, Mike slid a bottle and three glasses along the sloppy bar. Then, lowering his voice so it would not carry to the five men playing poker at a table across the room, he said warningly:

"If I was you, boys, I'd lay off that stuff, 'cause hell is sure goin' to pop here tonight. 'Stinger' Moore and his bunch is in town, old man Hill just slid in with a dozen of his gunslingers, an' there's a bunch from the Diamond A."

A stranger pushed through the swinging doors. The man gave one hasty glance around the room and headed directly towards the Bar L L Bar cow-punchers. As the three swung about to stare owlishly at him, he asked:

"You Toothpick Jarrick?"

"Yeh," Toothpick answered.

"Folks call me 'Tuscan' Blake." Then, leaning forward, he whispered in Toothpick's ear.

Toothpick exhaled his breath noisily and exclaimed:

"I'll be jiggered! The little runt is comin'!"

Tuscan Blake shot him a warning glance which silenced him. They had a drink together, and then Tuscan said carelessly:

"A gent tole me you might buy a couple of greys I got."

"Let's have a look at these here hosses."

Tuscan Blake nodded, swung about and, followed by Toothpick, clumped outside.

"That's them," Tuscan said as he pointed to the greys hitched to a ring in the side of the building. "Here's your bill of sale, and now I'm hittin' for Mexico, pronto."

"Is Jim-twi—" Toothpick glanced about him and decided to leave the name unsaid. "Is he headin' this way?"

"I don't know nothin'!" Tuscan cried, as he swung on a big, raw-boned sorrel. "He tole me to bring his hosses here, an' I brung 'em. An' I'm askin' you to remark that them greys is delivered in top condition! An' I'm tellin' you to keep 'em that way, unless you're aimin' to have a wolf camp on your trail!"

48

Toothpick nodded understandingly. "Ain't you goin' to feed befo' you go?"

Tuscan grinned and displayed a row of broken, blackened teeth.

"Not any! Two hombres is waitin' for me down the trail a bit. Towns ain't healthy for none of us!" With that, he swung his horse about and trotted down the littered street to the trail that headed south.

Toothpick watched him for a moment and then soliloquised:

"Now there's one tough gent, and I'm bettin' the two that's waitin' for him is the same, but here they come three hundred miles just to bring two hosses — 'cause The Wolf asked 'em to. Yes, sir, gents sure step high and pretty when that little runt speaks his piece!"

Swinging about, he stared at the two greys. Suddenly he grinned.

"I'm tellin' the world that you two hosses is still the meanest bags of bones on this here earth."

They laid back their ears and displayed their teeth when Toothpick approached to untie their lead ropes from the ringbolt. But as long as he did not come too near them, they followed him readily enough when he led them to the corral behind the hotel.

"You drunk?" Shorty asked Toothpick when he appeared in the bar a few minutes later. "Buyin' hosses from a gent like Tuscan Blake?"

Toothpick grinned.

"I got 'em right cheap; an' don't be laughin' your fool heads off, 'cause I got a bill of sale with 'em."

At this moment a man stuck his head in through the swinging doors and bawled: "Stage comin'!"

With one accord, everyone in the bar hastily downed his drink or laid aside his cards and trooped outside to watch the one big event of the day.

Old Tim, the driver, shouted to his sweating horses, the brakes squeaked, and the stage, with its enveloping cloud of dust, stopped. Men dressed in faded jeans, and booted and spurred, slouched from the bar and gathered to watch old Tim and his solitary passenger clamber down from the stage.

"Gosh almighty!" old Tim swore as he emerged from the dust cloud and stood blinking a moment.

Then he plunged through the door of the hotel and staggered to the bar. After he had washed his throat with three quick ones, he turned to those who had followed him and complained:

"I never seed such a kid! I've listened to guys that asked questions before, but that kid has 'em all beat. He's run away from home an' wants to be a cowboy."

"Reckon I got to give a look-see at that kid that can out-talk old Tim," Toothpick grinned.

He swung about and closely followed by Tex and Shorty, rolled to the door. When he first saw the object of the old man's wrath, he came to an abrupt halt and stared. At last he grinned broadly, turned to Shorty and said:

"He ain't overbig to be such a phenomenon, is he?"

"Let's see if he will scare!" Shorty grinned. But when he started forward, Toothpick grabbed his arm and rasped:

"Leave the kid be!"

The boy came over to Toothpick and Shorty and stepped between them.

CHAPTER
SEVEN

Nemesis

Ten minutes after Toothpick and the other Bar L L Bar cow-punchers had their first drink with the boy, he had them, as well as Mike, in a state of nervous exhaustion. They good-naturedly answered his questions when they could, for his likeable grin and ingenuous air had won them all. But he insisted on harping on the dangerous topic of the murders in the valley.

"But if you figure this Stinger Moore person is back of this stuff," he demanded, "why not cash him in? I thought you lynched folks like him out here?"

"Shut your gab!" Shorty pleaded.

"Sad-eye" Jones, a tall, slender man of twenty-five, who rode for old man Hill, cast a hasty glance about the room and protested:

"No one's sayin' they suspect Stinger."

But he spoke good-naturedly, for, curiously enough, although the boy shattered Western etiquette by his continual questions, no one became angry with him. He was a young man with whom nature had dealt kindly, for it had endowed him with one of those rare, irresistible grins.

"What's your handle, sonny?" Sad-eye asked.

"I'm Jim Ashford. I come from down Tennessee way. I'm goin' to be a cowboy."

Sad-eye reflected. He, as well as every other cow-puncher in the valley, had his own ideas as to who was back of the recent murders, and he realized the boy was a positive find. For the youngster, in the most innocent manner, was extracting various bits of information that the cow-punchers themselves hardly realized they possessed.

So Sad-eye listened with absorbed interest and with secret amusement to the obvious uneasiness caused by some of Jim Ashford's questions. Then it dawned upon him suddenly, that while the questions were apparently pointless and skipped about in a bewildering manner, when the answers, each in themselves harmless, were pieced together, they gave a complete history of the valley.

He chuckled when he realized that the cowboys, without knowing it, were undergoing a skilful cross-examination. Sad-eye glanced speculatively at Jim Ashford as he pondered:

"Has the kid a reason or is he just plumb curious?"

At last Toothpick interrupted the session.

"Let's rustle grub," he called.

"Do you know of a place where you can get —" The boy stopped abruptly.

"Ma Casey sure makes fine pies," Toothpick answered with a knowing grin.

With that, Toothpick, Shorty, Tex and the boy swaggered from the saloon arm in arm.

Sad-eye broke into a tuneless whistle as he watched them leave.

"Why did the kid stop, and why did his eyes flash when Toothpick mentioned pie? I'm bettin' that young one is a darned sight nearer twenty-five than he is fifteen. All right, Mr. Jim Ashford from Tennessee — Mr. George Hancock Jones is on your trail."

Shorty and Toothpick were leading the way to Ma Casey's, with the boy and Tex sauntering behind.

"Ain't he plumb marvellous?" Toothpick whispered exasperatingly to Shorty. "He gets you to speak out things in public you wouldn't dare whisper to yourself if you was alone in the Bad Lands."

Shorty glared at Toothpick.

"What's the matter with you? Did you come into money, or is you all set up 'cause that kid with his questions is like to get me gunned? An hour ago you was all full of gloom, and now you is all sunshine."

"Can you keep a secret?" Toothpick asked. Shorty nodded. "Nemesis has arrived in town!"

"Nem-e-sis?" Shorty took one look at Toothpick's grinning face and swore. "You go to Hades."

Many believed that Stinger Moore was a rustler, and that he was back of the murders that had held the valley in the grip of terror for the past six months. But no one voiced this belief nor searched too keenly for proof, for no one wished to be the excuse for another notch on those lightning guns.

Mrs. Casey, proprietress of Ma Casey's Eating House, had the needed expansive breadth to be called a motherly woman, but her hard little eyes staring out from a brick-red face gave this assumption the lie. She felt that fate had tricked her by taking Mr. Casey out of her life, and obliging her to turn her hand to work. She hated the country and avenged herself on its citizens by the sharpness of her tongue and the unpalatability of the food she served.

She flounced into the room and banged several plates before a customer with a take-it-or-leave-it air, then turned to Jim Ashford and the three Bar L L Bar cow-punchers, and awaited their orders.

Jim Ashford cast a despairing glance at the watery potatoes and greasy stew that had just been served his neighbour and humbly asked permission to wash up in the kitchen. Mrs. Casey's only answer was a glare but, taking this for consent, Jim hastily arose and vanished through the door in the rear.

A little later the rumbling roar of an angry woman swelled forth like thunder, and Shorty chuckled:

"I'm bettin' the kid comes out a-runnin'!"

"He'll be flyin', if he aims to keep ahead of the dishes she'll heave at him," Tex cried as he watched the swinging door with an expectant grin.

But the roar died away, and complete silence reigned, broken only by their neighbour's efforts to drink his stew.

A while later Jim Ashford walked to his place, gravely winked to his new friends and nodded towards Mrs. Casey, who followed with a large tray on which rested a big, juicy steak, flanked by canned corn and hash-browned potatoes. Stupefied, the cow-punchers stared at the repast, glanced at their own unpalatable stew, and asked:

"How did you do it?"

"Women is like hosses, and you got to handle them as such."

The cow-punchers grunted their disgust.

A moment later MacPherson appeared in the doorway.

"There's the boss," Tex cried.

Toothpick called:

"Come and get some real steak!"

Ian MacPherson, the owner of the Bar L L Bar Ranch, was a tall, raw-boned Scotchman of fifty. His big, bony head was covered with close-cut sandy hair. The long, drooping moustache that hid his tightly closed mouth was bleached by sun and rain to a pale straw colour.

"Mac, meet Jim Ashford."

The Scotchman extended a huge, thick-fingered hand to the boy, muttered a greeting, and fell to work on the steak. When he had finished more than his share, Toothpick seized the opportunity to say:

"Jim, here, is lookin' for a job."

Mac turned his shrewd, kindly eyes on the boy for a moment and shook his head:

"Too young!"

"But, Mister, I knows hosses and can do lots of things," Jim pleaded eagerly.

"Cookie's rheumatism is plumb bad. He tole me to get someone to help," Toothpick lied easily.

"Humph! All right, take you back with me tomorrow, but you got to stay close to the ranch and keep off the range." Mac gulped down his scalding coffee and then added angrily: "That white-livered sheriff won't do nothin', and the time's comin' when we'll have to clean out the nest of rustlers ourselves! Stinger —"

"You're talkin' loud, boss," Toothpick warned as he glanced hastily about the room.

Mac's eyes blazed with righteous anger, and he made the dishes rattle as he crashed his huge hand down.

"I won't be still. This has got to stop. Stinger's in town with his whole crew, and they're walkin' around with chips on their shoulders. They knows we suspect them, and I wants you boys to stay sober and keep out of fights!"

With that, he arose to his feet and clumped from the room.

"This Stinger person fast?" Jim asked.

"Chain lightning," Shorty averred. "He don't drink — don't do nothin'. He's quick and cold like a snake."

"Looks bad for Mac, 'cause a man could pick his teeth back and front before he could get that gun of his out. I calls it scandalous to squeeze a gun in a tight holster like Mac's." The boy shook his head.

"Say, kid, you're learnin' tricks fast." Shorty looked suspiciously at the thoughtful, freckled face opposite him.

"Say, don't you suppose they has guns in Tennessee?" Toothpick cried disgustedly.

CHAPTER
EIGHT

Snippets' Faith

The following morning MacPherson ordered Toothpick, Shorty and Tex to return to the Bar L L Bar home ranch immediately, nor would he listen to their protests that it would be dangerous for him to return later by himself.

"Buck and seven of his boys will be with me most of the way," Mac explained.

"I promised Mrs. MacPherson I'd stick close to you. So why not let us jog along with you all?" Toothpick queried.

"Yeh! And you boys so friendly with Buck's gunslingers," Mac said sarcastically. "Guns would be poppin' before we reached Big Buttes."

The three cow-punchers growled, but Mac remained firm.

"You bringin' that kid out with you?" Toothpick asked carelessly.

Mac answered shortly that, if the boy still wished to go, he would take him along.

Toothpick shot a quick glance towards Jim Ashford, who was sitting on the fence a few feet away. Then raising his voice, he said deliberately:

"There's only two bad places you got to watch — where the trail swings towards the Bad Lands, and when you get to the cottonwoods."

Shorty and Tex stared at Toothpick for giving this foolish warning, for Mac had travelled that trail many times before the lanky cow-puncher had ever seen it, and it was Mac who voiced their thoughts when he stormed:

"Don't you think I know?"

Toothpick grinned apologetically, swung on his pony, and said shortly:

"Let's go."

The three ponies were off like bullets with their riders yelling like so many madmen. Toothpick had passed the outskirts of the town before he remembered the greys. He yelled to the others, and their ponies threw up an avalanche of dust as they came to an abrupt halt; then they swung about and trotted back to the corral behind the hotel.

Swinging from his pony, Toothpick slipped through the bars of the corral and skilfully dropped his rope on the neck of the grey called Queen. But the moment he "sat on it", Queen charged towards him with bared teeth and chased him ignominiously over the fence where he was greeted by the jeers of Shorty and Tex.

"Mr. Tuscan Blake tole him they was broke and gentle!"

"An' he believed him," Tex chuckled. "He's sure gettin' simple-minded."

"He tole me confidential he got 'em right cheap," Shorty said gravely. "He paid two bits a head, an' I figger he got kind of stung."

"You grinnin' idjits! Hit the ground and lay your rope on that grey," Toothpick ordered.

"You watch us, cowboy, and we'll learn you how to rope a bronco," Shorty advised, as he and Tex entered the corral with their ropes in hand. Trailing their loops, they cautiously approached Queen from different angles. With great neatness, they dropped their ropes about the grey's neck. There was a snapping of teeth, a yell of warning from Toothpick, and Shorty and Tex appeared from a great cloud of dust, dived between the bars of the corral, and lay sprawling on the ground. And the grey went trotting about the corral with three ropes trailing from her gaunt neck.

"Why didn't you hold, you danged fool?" Shorty growled.

"Me? With that other grey kissin' my neck with her teeth?" Tex cried. "She would have sure bit my head off if she hadn't got ahol' of my hat the first snap."

"You say we ain't allowed to use our guns on them hosses?" Shorty asked. Toothpick shook his head. "Then you can ketch them yourself. I'm goin' to sleep."

Toothpick swore and ordered, but his friends resolutely refused to enter the corral unless they were allowed to go mounted and "bump" the grey — trip her with their ropes.

After the departure of the three cow-punchers, Mac had told Jim Ashford to meet him at the corral at ten o'clock, and he providentially arrived now to the assistance of the harassed Toothpick.

Jim slipped through the bars before he was seen, paid no attention to the cry of warning from Shorty, and headed across the corral towards the greys. The moment they saw him they charged straight at him. They squealed, pawed, and snapped at him, and then all were hidden in a cloud of dust.

"They'll kill him," Shorty cried. He yanked out his Colt and started forward.

"Don't start shootin'," Toothpick bellowed, as he seized Shorty's arm.

Then from out of the cloud of dust came the boy with the two greys trotting at his heels like two dogs. As the boy approached with their two ropes in his hand, Shorty and Tex had the air of men who have just witnessed a great miracle.

The boy grinned, winked at Toothpick, and said:

"Hosses is like women; you got to know when they're funnin'."

"Funnin'?" Shorty snorted. "How about grizzly bears funnin'?"

"Who's that jasper?" Jim asked sharply as he nodded towards a man across the street.

The man was in his early thirties, of medium height, stockily built and stout. He had a youthful, round face, soft-brown eyes, and smiling, thick lips. He was one of those men whom others like on sight and hail as a boon companion. Yet a close observer might have detected something about the eyes that somehow seemed to contradict the first impression, and the two low-hung guns were out of character.

"That's Buck Handscome, boss of the Diamond A," Toothpick replied. "He's runnin' more cows now than Mac."

61

"The Bar L L Bar brand shrinkin' and the Diamond A growin'?" Jim asked.

"Nothin' to that, Jim," Toothpick said hastily. "He works for a dude millionaire in the East, an' buys his new stock reg'lar."

"Sure?" Jim asked.

"Yeh," Toothpick replied. "He buys from the Hog Pen over in Colorado, an' each cow is vented proper. I helped drive in two thousand head this spring and see him pay for them."

"Aw, quit your jawin' and get goin'," Shorty pleaded.

With that the three cow-punchers swung into their saddles and, with Toothpick leading Queen and the other grey following close behind, started on their long, dusty ride back to the home ranch. Jim watched them thoughtfully for a moment, then turned and strolled back to the corral where he had been ordered to wait for MacPherson.

With apparent relish, the boy was watching the two hostlers harness Mac's half-broken ponies to the buckboard and was driving the men into a frenzy by his impossible advice as to how to accomplish their object. In the flow of language that issued from the two harassed hostlers, both Jim and the ponies were equally damned.

When Buck's eyes first rested on the boy there was a subtle change in the cattleman's manner. His hands hovered over his ivory-handled pistols and while the smile never left his lips, his eyes contracted and became mere slits. He moved with the feline grace of a panther ready to spring.

"Who is he?" Buck asked softly with eyes still on the boy and his mind searching the past for some elusive, mocking memory.

"A pilgrim kid I'm takin' out to help cookie," Mac answered.

Satisfied, Buck sighed, a long, hissing sigh, and shrugged his shoulders as if throwing off an oppressive weight. He laughed with a great relief as he said:

"Mac, you sure you hadn't better wait until tomorrow and travel with me and my boys?" Buck asked with apparent sincerity.

"No one will be knowin' I'm comin' out alone," Mac replied. Then his rage getting the better of his caution, he said angrily: "I'm not goin' to hide!"

Jim scrambled into the buckboard, and Mac nodded to the hostlers. They sprang clear, the ponies jumped, bucked, leaped forward, and were off with such speed that the boy would have been sent flying over the back seat if he had not been prepared.

The buckboard bounced and banged through the town so madly that the dust cloud it dragged with it held the ramshackle buildings in its embrace long after the buckboard had vanished upon the open prairie beyond.

A tall, awkward man dressed in soiled buckskins, whose face was covered with a tangled, matted, dirty beard, shook a clenched fist in the general direction taken by the buckboard.

"Damn ye, with yer airs and graces, makin' yer betters eat yer dust. Ye'll be eatin' it steady yerself afore sundown!"

"Time to hit the trail," announced a thin, wizened rider.

"The trail through the Bad Lands is seven miles shorter." The awkward one produced a bottle and prepared to take a leisurely drink.

"I said it's time to hit the trail!" the thin one rasped. The two others fawned at the menace in the professional killer's eyes, and the one with the bottle hastily returned it to his pocket and muttered:

"All right, boss."

They were well out on the sage-covered plain when Shorty suddenly turned to Toothpick and cried:

"We is prize idjits! Suppose Buck changes his mind and don't come with Mac?"

"If he does, Mac is just bullheaded enough to come by his lonesome," Tex declared. "They tried to get him twice, and I figure the third time will be sure pop."

Toothpick shrugged.

"The kid will be with him."

"Him!" Tex cried disgustedly.

Shorty and Tex stormed and wished to return to town for Mac, but Toothpick insisted he would be all right, and after a while the other two quit their tirade, and settled into glum silence. Suddenly Tex remembered a letter he had received that day.

"Got a letter from Pete Anderson," he informed them, "and he's plumb sore."

"What's he sore about?" Toothpick inquired, as he moved the wooden splinter that had given him his nickname to the other side of his mouth.

"He's plumb sore 'cause he rides a hundred miles up to Santa Fe to see a gent get his neck stretched, and the skunk breaks loose and plumb disappoints everyone."

"Huh! Too bad about him," Shorty snorted. "Who was the unobligin' gent?"

"One of them twins Toothpick was tellin' about — Jim-twin Allen."

"The one they calls The Wolf?"

"Yeh! The one what gives the locket to Snippets." He seemed in deep thought for a moment and then said: "Huh! Snippets told me she wrote and asked him to come and clean up this valley."

"Don't be lettin' her father know she done it," Toothpick warned. "Mac'd be sore."

"I hear tell that he promised to come, if ever she sent for him, 'cause she once saved his life when she was a kid — hid him in a wagon or somethin' when the sogers were huntin' him," Shorty volunteered.

"Do you reckon he'd come if she ast him?" Tex asked.

"You bet he'd —" Toothpick broke off. After a moment he continued: "I dunno. It was a long time ago."

CHAPTER
NINE

On The Trail

The half-broken ponies covered nearly four miles before they ceased their headlong gait and allowed MacPherson to ease them to a more moderate pace. The Scotchman had heard of Jim Ashford's inquisitiveness and was greatly relieved to discover the boy had that rare gift, knowing when to hold his tongue. Jim had sensed that Mac was not in the humour to talk and lapsed into a silence that was not broken until late that afternoon.

Mile after mile the buckboard bumped along the rough road. The dust was in their eyes, nose, and throat; the sun baked them. Seemingly Jim was suffering no discomfort from the heat, for his body was relaxed, and he was beating time with one finger on the stock of the rifle he held across his knees; while he hummed a Mexican love song and studied the open road with half-closed eyes.

The road turned sharply to the north and became rocky and rough as they climbed a hogback. Mac pulled the ponies to a slow, plodding walk and when they topped the rise, pointed and said:

"The Bad Lands!"

To the south-west lay mile after mile of tangled chaos — twisting gullies, deep arroyos with abrupt, crumbling walls — sheer, isolated peaks of sandstone, drab in colour and baked brown by the sun.

The road turned west, then south, as it skirted the Bad Lands, where they thrust a finger deep into the rolling plain. The boy glanced over his shoulder several times, then looked up at the Scotchman with a grin and asked:

"Is there a short cut across the Bad Lands?"

"Toothpick found a trail once, but he tried it again and got lost for a day." Mac drove on in silence for another mile, then looked down at his companion and asked: "Why did you ask about that short cut?"

"I was just thinkin' that if any gents was aimin' to bushwhack you, they would have to leave town after us, or they wouldn't know you was travellin' alone. And three hombres has been trailin' us since we left town."

Mac glanced hastily over his shoulder, then looked suspiciously at the boy and asked:

"How did you know there was three? Did you see 'em?"

"No," the other answered simply; "but I could count 'em by their dust."

Mac snorted.

The boy continued imperturbably:

"An' they cut into the Bad Lands back near them black buttes. By their dust, I reckon they're cuttin' across direct."

Deliberately, Mac pulled the ponies to a halt and stared out over the Bad Lands. He was proud of his sight, yet he could distinguish no sign of a dust cloud. He decided the boy was showing off, and said bluntly:

"Jim, you're lyin'! I hate boastin' liars!"

The boy reached down in his sack and produced a pair of field glasses which he handed to the Scotchman. The old man made a gesture as if to refuse them, but at the boy's quiet insistence, muttered something about "stupid foolishness" and levelled them at the distant horizon. After a moment he saw three faint, filmy dust clouds travelling across the waste. He handed the glasses back to Jim, whipped up his horses and said stiffly:

"I'll be takin' that back about your bein' a liar."

The sun dropped below the distant peaks. The waste of the Bad Lands became alive with glowing, vibrant colour. The giant hulks of the Big Buttes stood out against the painted sky like a mass of molten metal. The colours gave way to grey and then to black. The moon arose behind Beaverville and made the country black with shadows and silver with light.

As they were driving in the deep shade of some cottonwoods and willows an hour later, two deer bounded across a clear, moonlit meadow and, nearing the cottonwoods on the farther side of the road, turned swiftly off at right angles and went crashing through some brush.

"I reckon our friends are waitin' for us over there," Jim said softly. "Hop out, and let's fix a couple of bags of flour in them seats."

68

Leaping from the wagon, Mac lifted two bags of flour to the seat, where he stood them on end. After hats had been balanced on them and they had been wrapped in blankets, they made, in the uncertain light, excellent imitations of two sleepy men, slumped in their seats after a long drive.

Then Mac passed the long reins over the back of the buckboard, and he and the boy moved slowly forward, crouching behind the wagon as it entered the sheet of silver light that flowed between the two clumps of cottonwoods. Mac stooped to whisper a warning to Jim to stay close to him when the boy laughed suddenly — a joyous, wild, triumphant laugh.

That laugh was still ringing in Mac's ears when the shadows of the cottonwoods were cut by two streaks of flame. Mac's ears were deafened by the close reports as the boy fired three times in reply with incredible swiftness.

The shade was once again cut by the flare of a gun, and one of the sacks rolled to the ground. The ponies snorted with fear and bolted ahead. Mac tripped over a sack as he started in pursuit of the charging buckboard, and he fell heavily and rolled behind a patch of sheltering brush.

He heard a splintering crash as the racing ponies dashed the wagon against some tree within the shadow of the willows. With a sudden concern, Mac looked about for Jim and realized he had clung to the buckboard. With a muttered hope that the boy had escaped without serious injury, Mac considered his own position and grimly decided it was precarious.

69

He knew there were three men and they were sheltered, while he was in the open; for the bushes that concealed him were of no use as a means of protection.

When the next shot came from the willows, Mac exulted, for he observed that the firing was directed at the sack of flour that lay in the road. He crawled along a shallow washout which deepened rapidly towards the cottonwoods. Once there, he listened carefully and crept forward. A mumbled curse came to his strained ears, and someone called softly:

"Jumbo?" There was a silence and the voice muttered: "I wonder if the fool stopped somethin'?"

Mac placed the voice as coming from straight ahead and manœuvred for a position where he could get into action. Almost immediately he saw the man, standing in a little patch of thorn bushes. Carefully Mac raised his gun to his shoulder, but before he could fire, there came the sound of a shot, and the man gasped and sank slowly down. Again a crashing report; the trees flared red; a strangled cry! Mac whirled to see a dark figure fall forward and lie kicking convulsively in a small pool of moonlight.

"All right, Mac?" the boy cried as he stooped above the fallen figure.

"Ah, boy, 'tis glad I am to hear your voice!" Mac breathed with deep relief.

"That's the lot," Jimmy said carelessly as he turned the still twitching figure over and jeered: "Huh! Kitson!"

"Gently, man, don't be rough with the poor, misguided fellow," Mac reproved.

"Let's go see who the others are." Without hesitation, Jimmy led his unerring way through the trees to where the second man lay and unceremoniously dragged him into the moonlight.

"Know him?"

Mac shook his head, but he was able to identify the third as an ex-buffalo hunter, a ne'er-do-well, whom he had seen several times in Beaverville. Mac was astounded at the carelessness with which Jimmy killed and his scandalous disrespect for the dead.

To all appearances, the youngster thought nothing of having taken three lives that night. This was more than a boy's carelessness; it had a touch of the inhuman, as if Jim had the instincts as well as the eyes and ears of a predatory animal.

Mac had not lived on the border for several years without seeing many men killed, and he had known many killers during that time. But they had always displayed some sign of human emotion, either joy, hatred, revenge, or regret; never before had he seen anyone who killed like a wolf, thoughtlessly, remorselessly.

They found the runaway ponies and the smashed buckboard. As they came to the home ranch Mac's tearful wife threw herself into his arms as if she had feared she would never see him again. Mac's fifteen-year-old daughter, Snippets' welcome to her father was less demonstrative, but equally deep; she squeezed his hand, brushed his cheek with her lips, and her eyes told of a great relief.

71

As the boy stood and watched the two women fuss about Mac, the youthful expression left his face, to be replaced by one of infinite age as he turned and stared out into the night.

"Come here, Jim, and meet the wife and daughter," Mac called, but his tone was not cordial.

As the other stepped into the light, the woman cried: "He's nothin' but a boy."

"He's goin' to help Cookie. I've forbidden him to ride the range," Mac explained. "It was his eyes and ears that warned us this night and allowed us to circumvent them devils back there."

"If you have saved my man's life —"

"I'm not sayin' he did that," Mac, moved by his instinctive repulsion for the boy, interrupted dryly.

As two shadows materialised out of the darkness and reached out vague white hands for the ponies' bridles, he bade them see that the boy was fed.

Then he added to his wife: "Let's not stand here talkin'. I'm starved."

"The poor boy won't get anything from Cookie at this time of the night. He'll eat with us!" Mrs. MacPherson cried kindly, and impulsively seized the boy's hand and led him into the house.

Before the meal was half over, Jim's contagious smile and his friendly chatter had won both mother and daughter. And later, when they learned the minutest details of the fight, he won a still warmer place in their hearts. After he had finished eating, he rose abruptly and said: "I thank you for the food. Now I'll be turnin' in at the bunk house."

72

"I don't like him," Mac growled after the door had closed behind Jim. "He showed no emotion over them three misguided humans that died tonight."

Moved by some memory, by the sadness of the boy's face, Snippets leaped up and accused her father scornfully: "You don't like him, and he saved your life?" The girl stared at her bewildered father for a moment and then fled to the sanctuary of her own room.

"She is right, Mac," his wife cried. "You might at least try to hide the dislike you certainly have no reason for!"

"He's more wolf than human," the Scotchman declared stubbornly.

73

CHAPTER
TEN

Another Murder

The Bar LL Bar ranch house was a group of four buildings which formed a rough square. Built of thick, hewed logs, it was placed in a smooth meadow where there was nothing that could offer concealment for man or beast. For when it had been built, the thing of prime importance had been to construct it so that it could be easily defended in case of Indian attack.

Six years before, when MacPherson had driven ten thousand head of cattle into the valley the Ute Indians were on the warpath, the nearest town had been two hundred miles away, and old man Hill, who ran the Double S brand, had been his only near neighbour. Mac had cannily acquired control of the central and larger proportion of the water rights along Muddy Creek, by registering claims under the Mineral Lands Act as well as the Homestead Act. He had intended to obtain control of the water where Buck Handsome now had his Diamond A Ranch, but having entrusted the details to Haskill, his wife's foster brother, something had gone wrong, and he had been too late.

Preceding Buck's arrival two years ago, several small ranchers had moved into the valley, and with them had come Stinger Moore. The Scotchman dated all his troubles from the arrival of that sinister gunman. Stinger ran no cattle for himself, but went in for horses. His ranch was close to the sheer wall that separated the valley from the Bad Lands and was in the centre of a jungle of thorny brush.

Until the arrival of Stinger Moore, in spite of the blizzards and the droughts, Mac's herd had prospered, and increased by leaps and bounds. But during the past two years, every rancher in the valley had lost from five hundred to three thousand head. Everyone suspected Stinger, but no one had the least atom of proof that he had a hand in the disappearance of the cattle. Every possible trail from the valley had been watched, and yet the herds continued to dwindle away. How the rustlers got the cattle from the valley remained as much of a mystery as the murders that had terrified everyone for the past six months.

The following morning, Mac, a little ashamed of his unaccountable aversion to Jim Ashford, who had saved his life, wandered around to the cook house and found Jim listening to Cookie's wild tales of the old days.

The Scotchman was relieved when he saw, from the boy's friendly smile, that his ungracious conduct of the evening before had passed unnoticed.

"Mornin', Jim." Then he turned to Cookie and added: "Thought you needed someone to help, so I brought him out."

"Sure do!" Cookie spoke lugubriously. "My stomach is plumb bad."

"Huh! It's stomach now. Last week it was rheumatism from the hard life." Mac spoke bluntly; then he turned to Jim and commanded: "Remember, you stick close to the ranch, and the first time I catch you out on the range, I'll send you back to town!"

"All right; you'll never catch me there," Jim replied with easy confidence.

Mac considered this enigmatical reply for a moment. It might be taken to mean that the boy would obey orders and remain close to the ranch house, or it might mean that, if he disobeyed, he would take care not to be caught. Mac was a man of few words and blunt speech; his mind was not agile and he detested what he called "flipness".

He scowled suspiciously at the boy but could detect no guile in Jim's face. But as Mac stepped from the kitchen, and heard Jim shoot another preposterous question at the cook, he was not at all certain the boy had not been poking fun at him.

"The little devil, he has a deceivin' face, for all his honest smile and queer eyes!"

In spite of himself he chuckled at the manner in which Jim had inveigled the cook into telling tall stories which, if the cowboys once heard them, would certainly cause them to howl him off the range. Mac idly wondered why the boy was leading the cook on: he would have received an answer two days later, if he had happened to be present when the cook was violently berating Jim for having been absent from the ranch the whole day, threatening to inform the boss if it ever occurred again.

76

With a guileless air of innocence, Jim turned to Toothpick and two other riders and inquired casually:

"Did Cookie ever tell you about the old bad days in Dodge City?"

"Was he there?" Toothpick shouted; then, catching the wink Jim threw at him, he said: "I'd sure like to hear about it."

Several other riders eagerly chimed in for the story, and Shorty broke forth into roars of laughter at Cookie's apoplectic face as he frantically signalled to the boy to hold his tongue.

Later, Toothpick confided to Shorty:

"I'm bettin' Jim never peels another potato!"

He was right. A compact was arranged between Cookie and Jim that the boy could go and do as he liked as long as he whispered no word of Cookie's former wicked life.

So, while Mac believed Jim was safely peeling potatoes in the kitchen, he was actually riding the range from morning to far in the night. He sometimes rode the greys and sometimes a horse from the corral.

The horses were often turned back into the corral in a state of utter exhaustion, and once one had a long, bloody furrow on its shoulder. Toothpick cautioned the boss of the remuda to say nothing when that bow-legged puncher declared it was a bullet wound.

Then one morning "Big Ed" turned his pony into the home trail and was followed by another with a strange, dangling pack. A while later he pulled up at the bunk house and said laconically to Toothpick:

"Tex, down by the creek!"

Shorty and Jack White, a six-foot giant of a man, stepped through the bunk-house door and swore silently to themselves.

They were joined by others, until there were a dozen men in all — men dressed in faded jeans and torn shirts, with deeply tanned, unshaven faces — all staring at Tex, who had taken his last ride.

Something strange choked in their throats. They were silent and burned inwardly with a red-hot rage. Their very silence and self-restraint was a greater menace to the one whose finger pulled that trigger than if they had stormed and threatened.

"It's too bad," Jack White said softly as he bit a huge chew from his black plug.

"Tex could swear right pretty," Toothpick lamented as he unfastened, with deft fingers, the ropes that bound Tex to the saddle.

"Here's the boss," someone cried.

Mac, closely followed by Buck Handsome, pushed his way through the silent throng. When he saw Tex he burst into a torrent of profanity. He never smoked, chewed or drank, but, when aroused, his profanity was fearfully sublime and his ability to mix strange Scotch oaths with Mexican cuss words was held by the cowboys in reverent awe.

"That's the third within as many weeks!" He smashed his huge fist into an open palm with the noise of a pistol shot and stormed: "If that white-livered sheriff won't do nothin', I'll wipe out Stinger Moore myself!"

Toothpick warned:

78

"You're talking too much, boss."

Buck stormed and cried contemptuously to Toothpick: "Talkin' too much? If Mac won't, I'm goin' to end it. I'm not goin' to wait till another of my men is murdered. If we can't clean him out between us, why — I'll send south and get some real gunmen that have enough guts to face that murdering rustler and wipe him out!"

The implied slur made the cowboys flush angrily, and Big Ed moved forward menacingly.

"You can't talk that stuff to us. We ain't yellow. We'd have cleaned out that bunch of bushwhackers long ago if Mac hadn't a' kept us corralled, and you know it, too!"

A growl of assent arose from the others. Mac stepped forward, pushed the furious cowboy aside, and said:

"If I had not held you boys back you would have cleaned Stinger out a long time ago. Well, I'm not holdin' you back no longer!"

"That's the talk! Let's get goin' and send them to all hell!" Joyously, with many a wild whoop, the cowboys showed their appreciation. But their joy was short-lived. Jack Haskill, Mrs. MacPherson's foster brother, joined the group. He was a tall, thin, cadaverous man of fifty, dressed in a long, black frock coat. He cried sternly:

"Mac, remember what the Good Book says: 'Vengeance is mine.'"

So now, as they had always done in the past, these reckless words instantly sobered Mac. He stood in thought for a moment, and then he spoke to the cowboys:

"Leave things be now, and I'm promisin' you I'll end this thing one way or another." He swung about on his heels and clanked up the path to the ranch house.

On the rough veranda Mac found his wife and Snippets anxiously waiting for him. Mary MacPherson's natural volubility had been hushed by the constant fear that some day her husband would be brought home across a saddle.

"It's Tex," he informed her shortly.

"Oh, Ian, I'm afeared of the fourth time — they have tried three times. Let us go away! Buck can get us enough to live on for the rest of our lives. That dude millionaire will buy our ranch!"

"No," he answered sternly: "I'll let no murd'ring devil drive Ian MacPherson from his home. I'll be sendin' for the man who will stop these murders."

Buck swung about and asked Mac keenly:

"Who's the man?"

"Jack Allen!"

Haskill interrupted sharply:

"The man of blood — the twin brother of The Wolf?"

"Twin brother of the devil!" Mac answered heatedly. "The Cattle Association says he is the best man in the whole West!"

Snippets, a thin-faced girl, whose slender, wiry limbs were touched by the first roundness of coming womanhood, had been listening with eager, wistful eyes. A suggestion seemed to tremble on her lips, but she turned away and left it unsaid.

"If you're sendin' for anyone, why not get Snippets' bad man?" Buck sneered.

"I'll have none of his kind on my place. One is a bloody outlaw — the other a man of law."

"Father!" the girl cried.

"The Killer Wolf! He's well named, if half I hear of him is true!" Mac hewed to the line and was not prone to split hairs.

"He's the White Wolf," Snippets cried hotly. "Toothpick said he never shot a man unless he needed it!"

Buck smiled mockingly.

"Robin Hood! Why don't you send and ask him to keep his promise to you?"

Six years before, Snippets had discovered an exhausted man in her father's prairie schooner. Moved by some childish impulse, she had taken a liking to him, covered him up and, when some soldiers came to search the wagon, she was calmly sitting on the man, playing with her dolls. All that day she fed him and brought him water. When he slipped from the wagon late that night, he had given her a locket and told her, if she ever needed him, he would come and pay his debt to her.

Today she could no longer remember what he looked like and the image conjured by her imagination was far different from the reality. She was fifteen and in love with a memory, in love with a hero combining the best qualities of Robin Hood, Sir Launcelot, and Galahad!

The three men retired into Mac's office and continued the discussion of the best way to clear up the mystery. Haskill held forth hotly against Mac's hiring

Jim Allen's brother. He insisted that Jack Allen could not be trusted. But Mac remained firm and stubbornly insisted that he intended to send for Jack Allen that night.

"Huh!" Jim Ashford confided to Toothpick after the cow-punchers had dispersed and Tex's body had been carried into an outhouse. "Ain't it funny how Buck quiets down when that Haskill starts talkin'? If he's so anxious to wipe out Stinger, why don't he do it himself? He's got the men."

Toothpick nodded and looked thoughtfully at Jim.

"Funny how things fixed themselves to have Mac come out alone the other night."

"Funny, nothin'! I knew as soon as I saw that jasper Buck, that he had a finger in this pie!"

"You know him?"

"Yeh! But I ain't talkin' none now. How's Ma Jarrick, and how come you this way up here?"

"I don't know — itchin' foot. Ma's fine and keepin' a pie ready for you." After a moment Toothpick added: "How come you knew I was here, and has you learned anything yet?"

Jim ignored the first question.

"Yeh, I learns somethin'. So-long, I'm driftin'."

The boy swung on his horse. Toothpick watched him until he drifted out of sight. Then he growled:

"The aggravatin' little cuss!"

CHAPTER
ELEVEN

Jim Finds Out

The days slipped by, turned into weeks. Shadows lengthened, and the evenings became cool with the first signs of fall; and the Bar L L Bar punchers began their preparations for the beef roundup. Their outfits were overhauled and put in repair; ropes were limbered up, straps softened. Horses were given a few lessons of the sort which make a cow pony's education. And still, all day long and sometimes far into the night, Jim Ashford continued to ride the range.

One day Shorty sidled up to Toothpick and said:

"That kid is sure coverin' the range. One day I sees him up at Land's End, and the next Big Ed sees him over to Willow Camp. Why for is he ridin' promiscuous?"

Toothpick nodded casually and said:

"He's studyin' the *to-pography* of this here Murder Valley."

"*To-pog* — What the deuce —" Shorty abruptly broke off when he saw a pleased expression flit across his friend's countenance and added slowly: "Yeh, I reckon you're right."

At the first opportunity, Toothpick questioned Big Ed; for, while he would not admit it to Shorty, he was inwardly consumed with curiosity. He tried to give the impression that he was aware of the reason for Jim Ashford's long rides, but he was as completely in the dark as his friends.

Big Ed said:

"Since Tex cashed in, the boys has took to ridin' in pairs. Me and Jack White was gettin' grub when Jim pops up. He's plumb discreet and stays careful behind a rock when he announces hisself. He ain't no fool; he knows the boys is plumb nervous and is apt to shoot first and ast questions after.

"Jack is peeved 'cause the kid gets within pistol range before he shouts, and he says that the kid is takin' chances snoopin' up like that. But Jim, he laughs that fool laugh of his'n what makes folks like him, and he says he could've sneaked up and taken Jack's pipe out of his mouth without his knowin' it.

"We is both mad at this and tries to figure how the kid gets so close without us spottin' him. Jack, he says it's 'cause the kid ain't no bigger nor a peanut and can hide behind pebbles."

Toothpick sighed resignedly, for he knew better than to try to hasten the garrulous Big Ed, who, after thoughtfully rolling a cigarette, continued deliberately:

"Jim, he starts to ast questions, and we shows him where Tex got his. Then we points out where the sneaks hid when they drop'd him. He looks at the tracks, which is all mixed up. We starts laughin' and figger he's a fool tryin' to follow them tracks which is two days

84

old, but pretty soon we sees he's trailed 'em to where they left their hosses, and I'm risin' to state he's the best darned tracker I ever see.

"He points out that one hoss has an off front hoof that is splayed and that he passes a bit with his hind ones. We see four men ridin' hard to Widow Jackson's and later Jim, he finds the tracks of the hoss with the splayed hoof, so them fellows was the ones what handed Tex his ticket. And the fellow what was ridin' the big roan with the splay foot was 'One-eye', Buck's gunman!"

Toothpick whistled, then cautioned:

"Keep your trap shut!"

Big Ed nodded, and Toothpick sauntered around to the kitchen to question Jim Ashford. He found the boy sunning himself against the wall. He had a pail of potatoes between his legs and a paring knife in his hand. Toothpick grinned when he saw that not a single potato had been peeled.

"Say, Jim," Toothpick complained, "ain't it time you tole me somethin'?"

"Honest, I don't know nothin'. Leastwise, I ain't got no proof." He hesitated a moment, cast a quick grin at Toothpick and drew the Bar L L Bar brand in the dust at his feet: — L L — . Then added a few more lines and changed it to the Hog-Pen, barred like this: -L-L-

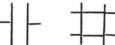

"But they was vented proper!" Toothpick exclaimed. "And I see 'em paid for proper."

"Maybe Buck owns the Hog-Pen and paid hisself!" Toothpick whistled.

"So that's why he takes me and some of the other boys with him when he goes to get them cows!" Toothpick gently swore at himself for his stupidity. "But how does he get 'em out of the valley?"

"Them cows fly out!"

"Fly out?"

"Yeh, they fly out. Just how they does or where I don't know, but I'm figgerin' to in a couple of days. Them cows fly out of the valley, the Bar L L Bar is blotted to the Hog-Pen, they is held somewhere till the scabs drop off, and then driven through the mountains to the Hog-Pen Ranch. Then after a time Buck, he goes to buy them, and they is vented proper, and you helps drive Mac's cattle to the Diamond A."

Toothpick flushed, and he said sadly:

"And me thinkin' I was plumb smart!"

The boy grinned at Toothpick's discomfiture and asked:

"How long's this gent Haskill been roamin' this range?"

"Him — that old sky pilot?" The contempt in Toothpick's voice showed he had no love for Haskill. "He turns up the year before Stinger. He fools Mac into sellin' him some water rights on t'other side of Muddy and starts the Tin-Cup.

"Mrs. Mac was plumb glad to see him; he's her foster brother and she hadn't laid eyes on him for fifteen years till he turned up here. She was right surprised to learn he'd gone in for preachin', 'cause she let somethin' drop that sort of showed me he was a hell-roller when she and him was kids back in Kansas.

"He says he'd ruther be killed hisself than to have blood on his hands, but just the same, he's got ten of the worst gunslingers in the valley that ain't so partic'lar."

"How come Mac to let Buck get the water in the lower basin away from him?"

"Mac was sore at that. He got Haskill to tend to that for him, an' Haskill was away buyin' the rights to that water hole when Buck shows up with the papers in his pocket.

"When Haskill gets back Mac jumps him for botchin' things and is tole that he has enough and that the greedy will lose all. It's darned funny how Haskill botched that thing. Buck sure outsmarted him and showed him up!"

"You sure?"

Startled at the thought that flashed through his mind, Toothpick stared at Jim for a moment and blurted:

"You don't mean —"

"I don't mean nothin', but I'm bettin' Mr. Haskill had another handle when he was down along the border. You know 'Slats' Foster and Sam Black down at Hollow Camp?"

"Yeh; Mac has 'em down there to sorta keep watch on Stinger Moore."

"You wait till Mr. Haskill is present, and then you go suggest to Mac they would be a heap more useful watchin' down by the Big Buttes. Mac thinks a heap of your knowledge, and you're right close to bein' the foreman of this ranch. So you press it hard, but not too hard, savvy?"

Toothpick had swung about and started off when Snippets came from the back door of the ranch house and headed across the court towards Jim Ashford. The boy held up a potato for Snippets' inspection and complained:

"Look at that thing! I sure wish St. Patrick had done away with potatoes when he killed the snakes."

Snippets laughed merrily.

"Why peel them? They're better in their skins."

"You tell Cookie that. He's a Dutchman and don't know nothin' a-tall about Irish spuds."

"You're a funny boy." Snippets studied him seriously, and her slender brown hand strayed to the locket that hung around her neck.

"Is that the thing The Wolf gave you?" Jimmy asked.

She nodded.

"He promised to come to me if ever I needed him. Do you think I ought to send for him now — to help Dad? Do you think he would?"

"Him! He's an outlaw — the Killer Wolf. Do you still think folks keep faith? He's prob'ly forgot you're alive."

There was no bitterness in his voice, but Snippets sensed it was in his heart. Their eyes clashed for a moment, and it was the boy who looked away first. She suddenly asked:

"How old are you?"

"Mac says I'm too young to ride the range," he replied as he picked up a potato.

The girl stood looking down at him for a moment, then said softly:

"I asked him to come. I *know* he will come!"

Jim seemed to have lost all interest in the outlaw and said:

"Cookie'll be skinnin' me if I don't skin these here potatoes."

Towards evening all the cattlemen of the district drifted into the Bar L L Bar Ranch for a big conference to discuss and appoint a captain for the coming round-up. Old man Hill, taciturn as usual, arrived with his foreman, "Dutchy". Doc Stewart and Buck Handsome arrived together just after sunset. Jim Hines, with a brother, and several of the smaller ranchers came a little later.

So it was not until after supper Toothpick found the opportunity he sought of seeing Mac and Haskill together. They, with Buck and One-eye, Buck's imported gunman, were closeted in Mac's office when Toothpick sauntered in. After twirling his hat in his hands for a moment, he said:

"Boss, we been losin' cows down near the Big Buttes. I got some traces of some rustlin' down there, and I was figgerin' it might be a good idea if we sent Slats Foster and Sam Black to kinda keep an eye on things."

"If you do less thinkin' and obey orders," Haskill said coldly, "we'd lose fewer cows."

Toothpick flushed and said stiffly:

"I was talkin' to my boss."

"You're doin' fine, Toothpick. I'm boss of the Bar L L Bar, and I'm satisfied," Mac soothed him.

Haskill exchanged glances with Buck and then relapsed into silence, and Toothpick went on to explain. But the moment he finished, and Mac decided it might be a good idea to send the two gunmen to the Big Buttes for a time, Haskill insisted they remain where they were.

"Those men were brought in special to watch Stinger Moore. If you take them away, you'll have to send others. And if they are killed, you'll have their blood on your hands."

"If you send two regular punchers to Hollow Camp, Stinger will get wise pronto. Them two hombres know their trade, which is watchin' for rustlers," Buck chimed in.

Mac looked doubtfully at Toothpick, who ended the argument by saying:

"Maybe these here gents is right, boss. At the Big Buttes, they would be right near town and very likely would be drunk all the time."

After Toothpick had left the room, the others talked for a time. Then Buck went out with One-eye, who was returning to the Diamond A. Outside, One-eye, after swinging on his horse, suddenly remembered something, leaned down and whispered to Buck:

"I just recollects. I sees that kid that's supposed to be helpin' cookie down by the Willow Camp. He was trackin'. We cuts down on him but misses him clean. You don't s'pose Mac is puttin' somethin' over on us?"

"That kid! Not any."

As Buck stepped on the rough porch to re-enter the ranch house, Toothpick passed him. Buck stared after the puncher for a minute, then muttered:

"I wonder if that fellow knows anythin'. He's sure actin' sorta mysteriously lately."

Toothpick glanced into the bunk house, saw that Jim was not there, and went on to the corral. Before he reached it a voice greeted him from the darkness.

"Over this way."

He found the boy perched on the top rail of the corral feeding the two greys and softly swearing at them.

"What you feedin' them bags of bones — pie?"

"Yeh! Cookie is plumb in love with 'em and makes a pie special for 'em."

Toothpick chuckled. He knew the reason Cookie made those pies — and it was not love for the horses but fear of the boy's tongue that impelled him to do the extra work.

Toothpick reported the result of his conversation with Mac and Haskill and asked:

"Why for did you want me to ask the boss to shift Slats and Sam?"

"I'm certain they's workin' with Haskill, and he's got 'em there for some reason he ain't tellin'." The boy laughed. "It sorta places where the cows start to fly outa the valley!"

After Jim had finished feeding his greys he asked:

"Do you think it's right, if you catch some fellows rustlin', to let 'em go, as long as you get the cows back?"

"It's right and then it's not," Toothpick replied cautiously. "It's up to the boss, 'cause a puncher works —"

"I ain't no puncher," Jim interrupted, "I'm a potato peeler, or supposed to be, and catchin' them fellows ain't my job. And I'm tellin' you plain — I says nothin' unless they gets off. They got nothin' to do with the killin's and they is only kids."

Toothpick pondered.

"Well, I reckon I could make enough noise to scare 'em away. But I *got* to have them cows."

"The Simpson boys is holdin' about fifty of Mac's cows in the hollow, back of Big Buttes." Jimmy broke off and called: "Don't be hidin' behind that post, Shorty."

A few seconds later a disgruntled Shorty loomed from the darkness.

"How the devil did you know I was there? I couldn't see you, so how could you see me?"

"I didn't see you, I smelled you."

With that Jim hopped from the fence, led the saddled grey from the corral, and followed in the direction One-eye had taken a short time before.

CHAPTER
TWELVE

Driven Out

About twelve that night Toothpick had gathered six punchers whom he could trust, and they were saddling their ponies for a raid on the Simpson brothers when three quick rifle reports sent them scurrying to the front of the ranch house. They were crowding through the door when they collided with old man Hill and Buck, who were rushing from the house with their guns in their hands.

"Some sneak bushwhacked Mac!" Buck cried.

"Shot him with a rifle from outside!" Old man Hill swore as he crowded by them and plunged into the darkness.

"Get your hosses, boys, an' get that fellow," Toothpick bellowed.

The punchers swung about, flung themselves on their ponies, and went crashing through the brush in ever wider circles.

It was Buck who discovered Jim Ashford jog-trotting towards the house with his rifle in his hand. Buck grasped the barrel, and finding it hot, snapped:

"What are you doin' out here?"

"Did they get Mac?"

"I'm talkin' to you! Talk loud! What was you doin' out here?"

"Me?" the boy answered coolly. "I was takin' a walk."

"All right, you come along to the house with me," Buck rasped. Then as old man Hill, Dutchy, the foreman of the Double S, and Toothpick materialised out of the darkness, Buck added: "Watch this kid. I finds him out here and his rifle is hot!"

Old man Hill asked:

"You don't mind tellin' us why you was out here?"

"Sure, I'll tell *you*," the boy said. "I was takin' a little ride — you see, I got to ride at night 'cause Mac don't let me ride the range — an' I was comin' back when I hears two hosses bein' led careful-like into that gully back there. I goes to investigate and is in time to see two gents cut down on Mac.

"I takes a shot at 'em and wings one, but he gets to his hoss and gets away. I was aimin' to get my hoss an' follow 'em when this gent grabs me. An' I guess them gents is away for good now."

They returned to the house where they found Doc Stewart soothing the distracted Mrs. MacPherson. Mac was lying on the couch with head bound up. He smiled grimly and said:

"It ain't nothin' but a scalp wound."

Haskill turned on Toothpick and snapped:

"How'd it happen you had six men mounted and armed at this time of the night?"

Flustered, the tall, lanky puncher hesitated and glanced at Mac, who, raising himself on his arm, said:

"Why an' where was you goin'?"

94

Toothpick cast an appealing glance at Jim Ashford and tried to evade the question. He was in doubt whether he had not played false to Mac and the punchers' code in promising to let the rustlers escape. He found it impossible to evade Mac's direct questions and blurted out the truth — that he was on his way to raid the Simpson boys, who were rustlers.

Oaths, a grinding of chairs as the ranchers leaped to their feet, a babble of questions and shouted advice.

"They must be caught — made an example of," Haskill cried savagely.

Five minutes later Jim Ashford, with a white, gaunt face, watched twenty riders clatter off along the trail to Big Buttes valley. He knew the Simpson boys were doomed — a rustler's fate, if caught, was sure. Every puncher carried a rope, and cottonwoods grew tall and strong along the creek.

He recalled the Simpson boys as he had last seen them — young, overflowing with spirit, with laughing, reckless eyes. He bitterly regretted the part he had played and was sliding towards the door to ride and warn them when Mrs. MacPherson spied him, and, mistaking the reason for his white, drawn face, said:

"Lands sake, I never did see a boy so starved lookin'. Don't Cookie feed you a-tall?"

A little hysterical over her man's escape, she felt like mothering the world, and pushed the reluctant boy ahead of her into the dining-room.

Mac, his head swathed in bandages, Buck, Haskill and old man Hill had not accompanied the lynching party; they entered the room and cut short Jim's efforts

95

to escape being forced to eat, while each minute, as it slipped by, more surely doomed the Simpson brothers.

As Mrs. MacPherson bustled into the kitchen, she called to Mac:

"You jist make him eat — the poor child looks starved."

"When mother gets set, you can't argue." Mac laughed loudly.

There was something about Jim Ashford that filled Buck with a vague uneasiness. He recalled how One-eye had said he had seen the boy down near Willow Creek Camp, and yet Mac insisted that Jim never left the ranch. Was Mac putting something over? Or was the boy deceiving Mac?

As Buck stuffed himself with food, he tried to stifle a premonition that he, as well as those who worked for him, were standing on the edge of a volcano. A sudden suspicion leaped to his mind, and he watched the boy carefully as he spoke to Mac:

"When's this here Jack-twin Allen due to arrive?" He sighed with relief, as he studied the freckled face opposite him and observed no sign of confusion.

"He'll be comin' shortly," Mac mumbled with his mouth full of hot biscuit.

"Why don't you get The Wolf, his twin — the one that gave Snippets the locket? Then you'd have a pair," Buck sneered.

"If you sent for him, he would come!" Snippets cried quickly.

"Will the child ever forget that foolishness? I wouldn't sleep a wink if that murderer was in the house," Mrs. MacPherson exclaimed.

96

"Is he as quick as they say?" Mac asked curiously.

"Ast Buck, here, if Jim-twin Allen is fast!" Haskill sneered. The boy caught an underlying taunt.

"Buck saw him kill four men in Tucson so fast they didn't have time to draw."

"I wasn't there when he done it," Buck snarled. "I've never seen him."

"An' I bet you don't want to," Haskill jeered.

"Maybe so. Yeh, he's fast," Buck said viciously as he glared at Haskill. "He's even faster than Jack Hart, the gambler, who used to be down on the border."

Like a flash from heaven the answer to many questions he had pondered over came to the boy.

It was half an hour later when he escaped from the kindly Mrs. MacPherson on the plea of a headache and fled to his horse.

The night was black, the trail through the Bad Lands unmarked. But it was seven miles shorter to the Simpson boys' ranch than by the other trail. Twice the rider lost his direction in the maze of twisting gullies and each time he cursed the darkness of the night. But at last he won through, and the grey, gaunt horse thrust forward her wicked head and sped through the darkness like a grey ghost.

Hammering at a locked door — a gruff voice in reply — a stone crashing through a window — a vanishing shadow in the darkness — a flare of a match in the cabin — a hoarse oath — a voice reading a note — " Hit the trail. The stranglers are coming."

It was nearly ten o'clock the next morning when the man-hunters, disgruntled, weary, hungry and thirsty, returned to the Bar L L Bar Ranch. Their nerves were raw.

One of Buck's punchers threw himself wearily into a chair and said:

"We found this. The rustlers got away."

Mac smoothed the crumpled paper and read:

Hit the trail. The stranglers are coming.

Frowning darkly, he stared about. No one could have known of the intended raid except those who had been present the night before. He realised, angrily, it was probably one of his own boys, someone who worked for him.

In the general, heated discussion as to the identity of the traitor and the steps to be taken to discover him, One-eye slipped through the door and whispered to Buck:

"Stinger says to get that there little runt who's s'posed to be helpin' Cookie. Stinger meets him comin' from the Bad Lands this mornin'. Then he must've gone to that gully and picked up my and Sam's trail and would have tracked us clean to the Diamond A, if he hadn't've run into me an' Stinger an' Sam an' Slats.

"We tried to get him, but he downs Slats an' gets away. We don't know who he is, but he's sure fooled us. An' Stinger says to get him an' get him quick!"

Buck's premonitions of the evening before returned with greater force. He knew now the boy was playing a part. His face grew black as he said:

"Where's that little runt that's supposed to be helpin' Cookie? He was seen comin' from the Bad Lands this mornin'!"

Mac recalled the boy's sudden headache of the evening before. Filled with quick suspicion, he sent for Cookie, who blurted:

"Ain't seen him since yesterday noon — an' he never peeled a spud nor done nothin' to help me since he was on this ranch — an' me with my stomach!"

But Mac had no wish to listen to Cookie's tale of woe, and he was unceremoniously pushed through the door.

"Is you talkin' about the kid with the freckled face?" a small rancher asked. "I see him the day afore yestiddy snoopin' around Ghost Meadow, an' he wasn't actin' natural, so I starts to question him, an' I'll be swanked if he didn't end by firin' questions so fast at me that I even tole him where I was born."

Haskill's cold, cutting voice stilled the hubbub:

"He calls himself Jim Ashford. Does anyone know if that is his real name? Does anyone know where he comes from or who he is? He warned these rustlers, maybe, because he is one of them!"

"Looks bad!" Mac admitted.

A roar went up from the wearied cow-punchers who had sought for so many lost cattle, and who had lost so many friends.

"Where is the spy?" One-eye shouted.

"Get a rope!"

Buck leaped to a chair and bellowed:

"You boys remember: shoot on sight — shoot him like you would a wolf!"

99

Mac opened his mouth to expostulate at this summary order when an unexpected interruption came from the kitchen. They all whirled to face the door as they heard Snippets' shrill plea:

"Don't go in there, Jim! They'll kill you!"

The door swung open and Jim Ashford appeared. For a second there was a stunned silence. His face was thin and pale and haggard from fatigue. His eyes met theirs unafraid.

"You gents lookin' for me?" he asked softly.

"String him up!" Buck cried.

"Kill him!" One-eye bellowed.

A scuffle, a clatter of feet as the enraged cowboys surged forward. Their very eagerness to be the first to reach him saved him. For no one dared to fire into that press. Mac's roaring voice cried:

"Stop! Stop!"

Snippets screamed:

"Big Ed! Toothpick! Shorty!"

Her appeal was wasted, for the three cow-punchers had pressed the boy in a corner and were shielding him from the eager, clutching hands of the enraged cowboys. A stentorian roar from Dutchy, the two-gun foreman of the Double S:

"I'll kill the man who touches the kid until he has his say!"

Old man Hill leaped into action. Throwing his weight this way and that he forced a passage to the side of Buck, who was standing on a chair, gun in hand, staring over the heads of the struggling punchers.

"Why for are you so anxious not to let the boy speak his piece?" he growled. And, from then on, the sleek, well-fed owner of the Diamond A ceased to take an active part in the proceedings.

He scowled at old man Hill, but holstered his weapon and stepped down from the chair.

When quiet had been restored Mac held out the crumpled note and asked:

"Did you warn the rustlers?"

"Yeh!"

"Did you shoot at me last night?"

"No!" Jim answered with a weary gesture.

Haskill interrupted:

"You warned those rustlers because you're in with them and were afraid they'd confess about you!"

"What?" Toothpick grinned into Haskill's cold face. "It was him what tole me about the rustling. He said they was only kids, an' he points out that lots of respectable gents throwed a long rope when they was young and frolicsome."

Several of the ranchers chuckled at this and nudged their red-faced companions.

"What are you afraid of?" Snippets cried shrilly. "That he will ride the range and find guilty tracks that lead to one of your ranches? The murderer that roams the range has reason to fear and wants to kill him! The rest of you are easily led, you blind fools!"

"I'm for lettin' the kid slide out, if he'll tell us what he is doin' here an' his real name," Doc Stewart spoke judiciously.

Old man Hill looked about the room from beneath shaggy eyebrows, and his eyes twinkled.

"That's fair, providin' we all tell him our real names. From the blushin' faces I sees about me, I reckon none of us don't want to do it. Speakin' personal, I've carried Hill as my handle for thirty years, but I ain't sayin' what I was called afore that!"

The tension broke, and they all laughed.

"Mac, I want to speak to you —" Jim Ashford began.

"I want to hear nothin' of you. You'll pack your sack and be gone," Mac answered sternly.

"What are you-all het up about? You got your cows back, an' the Simpson boys won't never bother you again. Why are you-all sore? 'Cause you-all missed a chance to do some safe killin'? Mac, you was all upset 'cause I didn't start cryin' about those men I downed in the cottonwoods.

"You was plumb horrified at me, and yet you get mad 'cause I warns the Simpsons and saves 'em from your ropes. You pass laws against killin' an' get your fun killin' the killer. You plumb gloat over a hangin' an' goes miles to see one!

"I fooled you 'cause I wanted to help you. My dad trained me to follow a trail, an' in a couple of days I reckon I'd have led you to a bunch of coyotes who really need killin' an' need killin' bad. That's all, I reckon. An' you can all go to hell!"

Mac's face was unrelenting.

"Hitch up the buckboard and drive him to town," he commanded Toothpick.

102

Buck stepped forward.

"One-eye is drivin' to town. He'll take the boy with him."

Jimmy returned to the bunk house and was occupied in rolling and tying his few possessions in a strip of canvas when Snippets appeared and pleaded with him. She talked rapidly for a few minutes but he shook his head. When he had finished his packing he threw his bundle over his shoulder, said good-bye to the girl, and started down the path to meet Toothpick.

"Jim, I'm right sorry. You ain't quittin'?"

"Don't you worry none. I gave a promise once, an' I ain't quittin' until I keeps it."

"You want me to drive you to town?"

"Not any; but you can kiss One-eye good-bye. He downed Tex!"

Toothpick shivered at the relentlessness of the boy's voice.

Jim whispered something to Toothpick and then went up to old man Hill. The two talked together for a while, and then Jim climbed into the buckboard beside One-eye and left the Bar L L Bar Ranch.

CHAPTER
THIRTEEN

Waiting

Just at dusk that evening Shorty and Big Ed led the two greys along the trail to the Double S, old man Hill's ranch.

"What's the idea of takin' these bags of bones to old man Hill?" Shorty grumbled.

"I dunno," Big Ed answered. "Toothpick sure loves to be mysterious."

"Ain't no livin' with him since he took to shootin' off big words." One of the greys balked at something in the road and Shorty jerked viciously at the lead rope. "Come on, dang you! If you was mine, I'd sure present you with a lead slug between them blasted eyes of yourn!"

"If what I suspects is certain," Big Ed said thoughtfully, "it wouldn't be safe for us to hurt them hosses, even if they et the shirts off our backs."

"How come?"

"I'm figgerin' they belong to that little runt, Jim, an' that he'll be turnin' up."

"Him! If I thinks he owns these here hosses, I'd sure drown 'em," Shorty snorted.

"If what I suspects is certain, then he ain't him but someone else," Big Ed said ungrammatically but emphatically. "An' if you has anythin' agin' him, I advises you to forget it fast!"

When they reached the lane that led to the Double S ranch house, Toothpick joined them and, after advising them to use their ears more and give their tongues a rest, led the way to the house.

Old man Hill was a bachelor, and his living-room showed all the disorder of the untidy male. A table littered with old catalogues, account books, pipes and bridles occupied the centre of the low-ceilinged room. At the farther end, several huge logs blazed in a rough stone fireplace.

Shorty and Big Ed, curious and wondering what this was all about, followed the example of the others and sought places near the fire. Old man Hill and Dutchy were renowned for their taciturnity. Toothpick stared into the fire and never opened his lips except to spit into the glowing coals. The five smoked in a silence which was suddenly broken by the stentorian snores of Shorty.

Growing impatient, Toothpick threw the door open and, followed by Dutchy, stepped outside. It was raining a fine mist, the night was black and the wind moaned softly in the cottonwoods.

"Do you reckon he'll come?" Dutchy asked.

Toothpick nodded.

They listened and were about to re-enter the house when the soft clank of a shod hoof against a rock

105

reached their ears. They cautiously walked towards the sound. A voice hailed them softly from the darkness:

"That you, Toothpick? Who's with you?"

"Dutchy."

A black blotch crept nearer to them, and the rider asked:

"Where can I turn loose this crowbait?"

Toothpick caught the bridle and asked in surprise:

"Where is your saddle?"

"One-eye didn't have one with him."

Unceremoniously the boy sauntered into the house, sank into a chair beside the fire, and called a greeting to the others. Presently Shorty opened his sleepy eyes and stared up at the little figure standing before the fire, sipping strong black coffee from a big tin cup. Shorty took one look and then rubbed his eyes and stared again.

This was not the boy he had known. The freckled face was the same, but it was older. And it was not the two low-hung guns that were "tied down" that made the change. It was something more subtle than that — almost as if the boy had thrown off a mask. In some way he dominated the room. He was no longer a laughing boy, but a man whom all there respected, and deep down in their hearts, feared.

Jim spoke:

"I get the history of this here valley this way: Six years ago Mac drives in ten thousand head, and he and Mr. Hill has the whole place to themselves. Then Haskill turns up, and Mac turns over to him some water rights. Then Stinger Moore comes, and cows

106

start to disappear. Buck comes next, drivin' a lot of Diamond A cows, which he says he bought from the Hog-Pen across the line.

"They is the cows Stinger rustled — it's plumb easy to fix the Bar L L Bar to read Hog-Pen — but they is vented proper, so no one is suspicious. But everyone is Mac's cows. 'Tain't easy to blot the Double S, so they sells them cows across the line as beef.

"Then Tex and the other boys gets cashed in, but that's just incidental to the rustling. They was all A-1 punchers, 'cause they could read brands and trail. Well, they learned somethin' and tole it to someone they thought had a right to know. So they was gunned!"

"How do they get the cows out of this here valley?" old man Hill demanded.

"They make 'em fly out."

The boy grinned weakly, staggered and caught Dutchy by the sleeve. He wavered a moment and then slumped to the ground.

Big Ed lifted the fainting man gently and cried: "He's creased!"

While Dutchy hastened to get a carefully hidden bottle of rum, Big Ed and Toothpick removed the stained shirt and stared. There was a long, jagged wound across the boy's chest.

"Great jumpin' cats!" Shorty cried. In telling a friend about it later, he said: "You couldn't've laid your open hand on his chest without touchin' a bullet wound or a knife scar."

Under the potent influence of Dutchy's rum, the unconscious man's eyes fluttered and opened. He

107

explained he had been tracking the men who had shot at Mac the evening before when he had been jumped by One-eye, Stinger Moore, and two others. In the running fight that followed he had shot Slats Foster and received his own wound.

"Did you have it this mornin' when them coyotes was cussin' you?" old man Hill asked. The boy nodded.

"Who is he?" Shorty asked in an awe-struck whisper.

"The Wolf — Jim-twin Allen!" Toothpick said in reply.

The following evening twelve heavily armed riders left the Double S Ranch and headed towards Stinger Moore's and the Bad Lands. Old man Hill and Jim Allen rode in the lead, with Shorty and Big Ed close behind them. Following them were ten hard-bitten punchers, the pick of the Double S fighting men.

About the same time four other men, riding in pairs, swung their horses towards the famous gunman's ranch.

Four hours later the first group of riders rode slowly through the broken land that lay west of Stinger Moore's ranch. They rode silently, with no sound except the occasional clink of a shod hoof against a flint rock or the swish of a scraping brush against chaps.

They travelled in single file, and the blackness of the night was so deep that each one could see only the blur of the rider preceding him. Somewhere a cougar snarled, or there was a crashing noise as some animal went blundering through the brush.

Jim called a halt and said:

"We're gettin' close. Stinger's place is about half a mile to the left. I'm goin' ahead to see if things is all right. I'll give a wolf's howl three times, then you-all come on." He swung from his pony and vanished in the darkness.

"It's sure dark," someone complained.

"He can sure see in the dark," Dutchy answered. "Did you see his eyes? They was yellow like a wolf's."

"Huh!" Shorty chuckled. "Won't we be tellin' things to Toothpick about cows flyin', an' him sent back to dry-nurse Mac."

They grew silent, lolled in their saddles, and strained their ears to catch the first signal. Off to their left a wolf cried, to be answered by one on their right. Once, twice, thrice it mourned.

"That's him!"

Shorty shivered.

"Which one?"

Carefully they led their mounts forward, and in a few moments Jim Allen materialised out of the darkness.

"We're right close to Stinger's place," he whispered.

He led them forward to a deep, bowl-like depression with shelving sides. Here he turned to old man Hill and whispered:

"You come with one of your boys, an' I'll take Big Ed. We got to climb, so it's no use toting rifles." Turning to Shorty and the other disgruntled riders, he added: "If you hear gunnin', get those hosses unhitched."

Dutchy, Big Ed, old man Hill and Allen clambered out of the depression and went towards the high wall

109

that separated the Bad Lands from the valley. Reaching this, Allen whispered:

"This is the place."

Jim fastened two ropes together. Climbing noiselessly and rapidly, he vanished into the dark above their heads. Five minutes later the end of a rope switched across their upturned faces and, one after another, they seized it and dragged themselves to the top. When all three had joined Allen, he led them forward a short distance, crouched in the shelter of some brush, and warned:

"We got to wait now. That wind is goin' to blow them clouds away an' it'll be lighter, an' then you'll see how cows fly!"

About two hours before Allen and the Double S riders reached the cliff, Buck, with a thin, wizened man, followed by two punchers with rifles slung across their saddles, picked their way through the dense brush that masked Stinger Moore's ranch. Sliding from their ponies, they were met by Stinger.

"Come in, gents, and have a snort of liquor."

With his low-hung guns flopping at every step, he turned and led the way into his office. The four men clumped in after him and each seized a glass of the fiery liquor. Then the thin, wizened man turned to Buck's guard and ordered:

"Get out!"

After the two guards had left, the three remaining men eyed each other suspiciously. Finally the thin man snapped:

110

"You sent word you want to quit. Why?"

"Well, I've been —" Stinger began.

"Gettin' cold feet!" Buck interrupted with a sneer.

Stinger's expression did not change, but his eyes narrowed as he answered:

"I wouldn't be talkin' that way, Buck, unless — unless you're really figgerin' on findin' out which can throw a gun the quicker!"

As he met Stinger's cold, expressionless eyes, Buck's filled with the lust of the natural killer. His was a temperament that could not abide anyone who questioned his superiority, and he felt the urge to settle the question of pace now.

Stinger was another type of fighter. Cold, passionless, he took no pleasure in killing. Yet he would kill as quickly and ruthlessly as Buck. But there must be some measure of gain before he would put hands to a gun. The third man combined the instincts of both the other two and was the most dangerous of the three. If possible, he was more unscrupulous than the others, and he now interrupted them in a voice that was as chilly as ice:

"I'll drop the first man who reaches for his gun. I'm playin' for a big stake, an' I'm not going to have my chances spoiled by either of you. The worst of you gunslingers is that you're cursed with a suspicion that someone else may be better than you, and you can't sleep until you find out." He added contemptuously: "An' you kill more men among yourselves than the sheriff ever gets."

111

The tension relaxed and the killing light died from Buck's eyes. He spoke conciliatingly:

"I guess there are three men who are faster than anyone else in the world: Jack Hart, 'Black Dick', and Stinger Moore."

Jack Hart, the tall, thin man, nodded, but Stinger disagreed:

"I dunno — those twins —"

Jack Hart interrupted:

"What makes you want to quit?"

"Well," Stinger answered thoughtfully, "I've got me a tidy stake, an' we've had luck. Time's comin' when it's goin' to change, an' I ain't aimin' to be here when it does. An' I don't like that kid gettin' loose. He knows somethin'."

Jack Hart nodded.

"You're right. We got to finish up quick. Stinger, tomorrow you have your boys drive the cows to Lost Canyon an' hold them there. Stop slingin' any more; chop up the crane; burn up everythin'; clean up tracks! I'm goin' to get Mac."

"How you goin' to get him?" Buck asked. "He never moves out less'n he has five or six punchers as a guard."

The three entered into an animated discussion as to the best way of removing Mac, the last obstacle to the realisation of their dreams. Finally they reached a decision.

"Then that's settled, an' it's sure neat," Buck cried.

"S'posin' he won't go, or takes a bunch with him?"

Buck laughed.

112

"Talk to Mr. Haskill — he'll make him go."

Stinger seldom smiled, but he evidently found this a good joke, for his eyes flashed and his thin lips cracked in a fleeting grin.

"Mac reaches town, we take him to Silent's place, tell him we got proof Stinger's been rustlin'; Mac gets excited, makes threats; Stinger comes in an' stings him."

"An' after?" the killer questioned.

"You take to the Bad Lands. You can work around to this place or go to the Lost Canyon until things blow over."

"Nope!" Stinger shook his head decisively. "They might start chasin' me, an' I don't want a bunch of eager cowboys throwin' lead at me. I stays in town; you both swear he drew first; Silent does the same. I'll let him get his gun out before I goes for mine."

Later that night, when Buck and Jack Hart were driving away from the ranch, Buck remarked: "Too bad you consented to let Stinger stick in town after the killin'. Sort of looks bad for us if we don't make no move."

"We're goin' to. I'm figgerin' it'll make our hand stronger if, *after* Mac passes, we help Stinger cash in his chips!"

Buck whistled with admiration at this bold stroke. No one would connect them with Stinger's rustling if he died in this way.

"Just before Stinger arrives," Hart went on, "I go out to Levy's Emporium. I hear guns, rush back, hear that Stinger has killed my foster sister's husband — an' drop him!"

CHAPTER
FOURTEEN

Queen's Death

Waiting is the most trying ordeal for the nervous, active man and, as the long hours passed and nothing happened, Big Ed became impatient. The wind drove the low, hanging clouds away, stars dotted the heavens, and the impregnable darkness lifted. He rolled towards Allen, who was lying flat on his stomach, asleep. The lanky cow-puncher edged towards Dutchy where he whispered his disgust.

"He tole us to keep our ears open an' the little runt is fast asleep."

As he watched, Allen raised himself on his elbow, his head rolled from side to side for a moment, then remained fixed as the eyes stared past Big Ed's shoulder into the blackness of the Bad Lands. The cow-puncher knew something had aroused Allen and concentrated his own gaze in the direction in which the outlaw was looking. But Big Ed could neither see nor hear anything.

Allen whispered:

"They're comin'! Tell the boys."

Two minutes passed, and still the others' straining ears could catch no sound. Then there came the click of horses' hoofs and the low hum of voices. With tense nerves and straining ears Big Ed listened. He gave a gasp and stared, for suddenly a bawling cow hung suspended in that lighter line where the sky met the top of the cliff. With rapidly moving legs, it swayed off towards, and vanished into, the darker shadows of the cliff top.

Recovering from his astonishment, old man Hill whispered to Dutchy:

"That's how they get the cows out of the valley — easy as pie."

"A derrick, a block and tackle, and a team of mules, and the cows fly over the rim," Dutchy chuckled. "Just like they load 'em on steamboats."

For an hour they lay there and watched cow after cow swung up over the rim of the cliff. Then a creaking of leather warned that the men were mounting. A few shouts and the stolen cattle were driven away into the interior of the Bad Lands.

After the four had slid down the cliff and rejoined the others, old man Hill said:

"We sure got Buck, if we can find where they hides them cows, 'cause their blotted brands will be green."

"We'll find 'em," Allen stated confidently. "An' I'm trustin' you-all won't let none of them fellows get clear to warn their boss."

"Buck or Stinger?" Dutchy questioned.

"Neither — a gent what used to call himself Jack Hart."

About noon of the following day, a horseman riding in advance of several others, topped a rise and let out a yell of greeting when he saw Toothpick:

115

"Good news, cowboy! There ain't no mystery, and this here valley is goin' to be mopped up clear like a kitchen floor. I'm tellin' you — we seed cows fly, and then we jumps the rustlers what was holding three thousand head in the Bad Lands. Seven of them, an' they all dies with their guns in their hands. Big Ed gets nicked and Tom Harris gets his ticket. Then we jumps Stinger's ranch an' gets two more. We're goin' to gather the ranchers and mop up Buck's ranch. Where's Mac?"

"Mac, he went to town with Buck an' Haskill!"

Allen had come up to Toothpick and Shorty and he asked sharply:

"How long ago? How come he went with them?"

"Haskill tole him he had proof of Stinger's rustlin', an' they went to get the sheriff."

"Toothpick, I'm borrowin' your horse. Get some fresh horses an' some men an' follow me to town. I'll mark a trail for you through the Bad Lands. Hill, take your men from Stinger's place. We'll do our moppin' up in town!" Allen turned to the big roan and called: "Come on, old lady!"

He trotted down the lane and turned into the trail to Beaverville. He pushed the roan into a long, swinging lope and, with Queen following closely, dipped from sight behind the hill. The others watched him until he disappeared, and then Dutchy cried with an oath:

"I ain't goin' to let him go alone!" Swinging his winded horse about, he started in pursuit of Allen.

It was twelve miles, as the crow flies, to the entrance of the Bad Lands. Here Allen was forced to swing on the back of Queen, for the big roan was blown and

116

exhausted. He never faltered as he made his way through the twisting gullies. As he went, he marked the trail clear and plain for Toothpick and the others who were to follow.

"Come on, you bag of bones!" Allen swore softly as he emerged from the farther side of the Bad Lands. "Put your best legs forward, 'cause I has a feelin' this is our last ride together!"

The gaunt grey pricked up her ears, thrust out her wicked head, and settled into a long lope that devoured the miles.

The last ride of Allen and Queen was to become a legend in horse annals. Queen was far from fresh; she had followed the roan until he cracked and had travelled hard the day before. Once the old horse faltered in her stride, and Allen leaned forward and encouraged:

"We gave a promise a long time ago an' we got to keep it. Get on, old lady!"

The town was in sight before she faltered again. Allen's face was old and haggard, for he knew that Queen's heart was close to breaking. Still he encouraged her. Again Queen responded. Then, as the outskirts of the town were reached, she slowed to a panting walk. Allen slid from the saddle as Queen gave a shudder and slowly sank to the ground. Mouth open, her eyes bloodshot, she gave a great sigh and lay still.

"Good-bye, Queen!" Allen spoke softly. "You was old an' you sure died a hoss's death."

He stood looking down at her for a moment, then turned away. Several spectators moved up, but,

117

catching a glimpse of his face, left their questions unasked.

Allen went directly to the Lone Star Hotel, where he learned that Mac and Haskill had left for Silent's gambling house. Heading directly to the resort, Allen slipped around to a side door and peeped in. He saw Mac, Buck and Haskill sitting at a table near the front entrance.

He slipped in, selected a table in a curtained alcove, and sat down and waited. He knew that Mac would not listen to him, even if he could separate the Scotchman from the others; so the only thing for him to do was to wait and let the plot develop before he took a hand. A few minutes later he heard Mac cry angrily:

"If you have proof and the sheriff won't act, then I will get Stinger Moore myself."

Buck and Haskill leaned forward, and Allen caught the triumphant look in their eyes. He knew that Mac would have the chance of a child before a ruthless Indian, if it came to gun play between the Scotchman and Stinger, for Mac possessed none of that lightning-smooth co-ordination of brain and muscle that was so necessary for the gunman. He was deplorably slow, and his eyes would telegraph seconds ahead his intention to draw.

At that moment a girl approached Jim Allen where he sat alone.

"Hello, boy, you look sad."

Partly because the scrawny little slip of a thing, with her child-like face and old woman's eyes, touched a chord of sympathy in his heart — for they were both outcasts — and partly because he thought he would be less conspicuous sitting with her than alone, he said:

"Sit down, sister, and have something."

Drinks were ordered from a pock-marked waiter who over-charged Allen. As he made no protest, the girl said:

"Seein' as you're a millionaire, you might slip me somethin'."

Allen carefully divided his slender roll and gave half to the wondering girl, who looked with puzzled eyes at the freckled face opposite her. Then, sensing a sympathetic listener, she poured out her sordid history — a commonplace tale enough, of a man who had brought her here, and grown tired of her. It was impossible for her to save enough money to leave.

"There's the man now," she said, pointing at Buck.

Allen made no answer, for Haskill had turned and walked out. Almost immediately Stinger entered. His mouth a thin slit, his eyes cold, he walked directly to Mac and said:

"Hear you're lookin' for me! Hear you got somethin' to say!"

Believing Haskill had gone for the sheriff, Mac curbed his temper and spoke abruptly:

"I'll be talkin' to you shortly."

"The dirty swine is goin' to kill that man!" the girl whispered to Allen.

"Well, if you got somethin' to say, say it now — 'cause I'm goin' to start sayin' things to you," Stinger said cuttingly. "You can't call me a rustler. Take it back or go for your gun!"

119

Bewildered, Mac slowly arose to his feet. He glanced appealingly at Buck and was puzzled at the hardness in his friend's face. Allen rose slowly to his feet, and shook off the girl's detaining hand.

"You fool, they'll kill you!" she cried in warning.

Then she thrilled as she caught the yellow flare in his eyes and heard his low laugh as he went towards Stinger on stiff legs like a fighting wolf.

"Mac, I'm tellin' you, either take back what you said or talk public an' say you're a liar!" Stinger cried.

Thrown off his balance by the suddenness of Stinger's attack, Mac again looked appealingly at Buck. It was then he understood, knew that Buck was not his friend, and that, if necessary, the boss of the Diamond A would aid the gunman.

Mac knew himself to be no gunslinger, knew that he had one chance in a thousand; but he had the bravery of his race and intended to make a try for that one chance.

As he moved forward, Allen knew he must turn the attention of both Buck and Stinger towards himself. The main thing was to drop them both before they got Mac.

"Kid, you keep out of this," Buck warned sharply as he recognised Cookie's ex-assistant.

"Black Dick, don't you know me?" Allen laughed as he swayed slightly on his toes.

Startled, Buck stared at Allen. The blood drained from his face and left it ghastly white as he whispered:

"The Wolf!"

120

For a second, Stinger and Buck stared as if suddenly confronted with the ghosts of all their past victims. The girl laughed hysterically. Without understanding, Mac watched the hard, sneering, malevolent triumphant look wiped from his foes' faces, to be replaced by one of startled fear.

A voice called:

"I'm countin' three!"

Frantically Mac reached for his guns as the others went into action. Dense clouds of blue smoke cut with continuous jagged flames! A moment he was standing before him; a startled look sprang to the man's face and he slumped to the floor with a smoking gun in each hand. Silence!

The swinging door opened, and Haskill entered. A scene so different from what he had expected momentarily threw him off his balance. But he quickly recovered his wits as a small, swaying man crept towards him and called softly:

"Jack Hart, I'm countin' three!"

The yellow, flaring eyes told him who stood before him, and Haskill's right hand flashed to his hip and his left to the gun in his shoulder holster. But he was not fast enough; an infinitesimal atom of time spelled death. His right gun came free and flared as a slug tore into his middle. He staggered backwards and toppled through the swinging doors into the dusty street.

Mac stared stupidly as the swinging doors banged shut. Then he saw Allen stoop quickly, thrust a hand beneath Buck's blood-stained shirt and pull forth a money belt. He tossed it to the girl who was standing by a table and said:

"Reckon that'll shore take you away!"

Allen swung about. As several men rushed through the front doors, he slipped quietly through the rear.

Meanwhile Toothpick had no difficulty in finding the trail through the Bad Lands, and he and the Bar L L Bar riders approached town a short hour after Allen had arrived.

"Ain't that Jim's grey hoss?" Dutchy, who had been overtaken by the others, pointed to the sprawling body of the grey.

"He rid her to death." Toothpick alone realised the extent of Allen's sacrifice and added grimly: "Somebody will pay for it."

As they neared Silent's gambling hall, the roar of five Colts greeted their ears and, as they sprang from their saddles, they saw Haskill rush from Levy's Emporium, run across the street and push through the swinging doors. As the Bar L L Bar boys, guns in hands, raced forward, they heard a laughing voice call:

"Jack Hart, I'm countin' three!"

As the cow-punchers reached the saloon, Haskill, wreathed in blue smoke, staggered backwards through the doors and collapsed in the road.

Mac was still staring at the prostrate bodies when he heard Toothpick exclaim behind him:

"He got all three!"

Mac nodded and moved to the door. The crowd of roughs, who had hastened like vultures to the scene,

122

gave way. For they all believed then, and some do now, that Mac had killed the three gunmen single-handed. Mac was too bewildered by the shock and horror of it to tell the story then, and, when he told it later many refused to believe him.

Later Toothpick got the true story from the girl, and it was while he was talking to her that he learned the value of a name. Silent, the saloon keeper, abruptly ordered her to hand over Buck's money belt, and she replied:

"*He* gave it to me."

"Who?" Silent snarled.

It was Toothpick who answered:

"Jim-twin Allen."

Silent turned and walked away.

CHAPTER
FIFTEEN

A Decision

Toothpick Jarrick snuggled deeper into his slicker and gently swore at himself. Saving a short halt at the noon hour, he had been in the saddle since five o'clock in the morning and now five had come around again. And all day it had rained, a steady downpour that turned his hat into a soggy mass of felt, that trickled down his neck, and ran from his slicker to fill his boots.

"Huh!" he grunted as the rain defeated his efforts to fashion a cigarette. "Toothpick, you're sure a prize fool, turnin' yourself into a web-footed fish, chasin' a runt halfway round the world."

Far in front the foothills rose through the veil of the rain, indefinite and mysterious; behind them the Tetons towered, their peaks hidden by the low-hanging sullen clouds; and nearer, dark and blurred by the rain, a clump of cottonwoods stood out suddenly in the vast, wet plain.

With a sigh of relief, Toothpick turned his tired pony straight towards them, for there — unless he had lost his direction — food, shelter, and warmth awaited him. As he neared the ruined buildings of an old ranch just to the left of the cottonwoods, he pulled his pony down to a slow walk, dashed his hand across his eyes to free them from the beaded drops that clung to his lashes, and stared long and hard at the old buildings.

"I don't care if the place is plumb full of horse thieves, I'm goin' in out of the rain," he muttered between chattering teeth. Then, lifting his voice, he called: "Hallo!"

As the moments slipped by, and the silent buildings gave no sign of life, Toothpick loosened his slicker and threw it back so it no longer concealed the Colt that hung at his hip. Then a door gaped open and a tall, powerfully built, swarthy man appeared and grinned a greeting at him.

" 'Lo, Dutchy," Toothpick cried as he swung from his pony.

"There's hay in the lean-to. Just got here an' am makin' a fire." With that, Dutchy turned and vanished within the dim depths of the house, and the tall, gawky cow-puncher led his pony to the lean-to. As he was unsaddling, he grunted to himself:

"Dutchy sure talks like words hurt him. I've rid nigh on to two hundred miles to meet him here, an' ain't seen him for a week, an' he don't even say how's your health or is you wet."

Having attended to his pony, Toothpick splashed his way through the wet, clinging mud to the front of the house. Throwing open the door, he was greeted by a welcoming blaze, for Dutchy had the fire going and was busy with a frying pan and coffee pot. Supper was eaten in total silence. Then, after each had gorged and both were puffing at a cigarette, Toothpick grumbled:

125

"Huntin' for a needle in a haystack ain't nothin' to huntin' for a gent — an' him not full grown — in this country."

"There's only one underground trail through the Tetons, an' Jim Allen will sure be takin' it," Dutchy grunted; then he sank back as if exhausted by this unusually long speech.

"One!" Toothpick exploded. "Ain't I back-tracked an' hunted along a dozen?"

"There's only one," Dutchy repeated. "She splits and forks a trifle, but she's only one." And to end the discussion he pulled off his boots, placed them before the fire to dry, rolled in his damp blankets and, a moment later, announced he was asleep by a loud snore.

"Dutchy may be sure enough a fightin' son of a gun," Toothpick grumbled as he prepared to follow the example of his companion, "but he sure ain't no gent to take along with you where it's so darned quiet it hurts your ears."

Ten days before the two had left the railhead in Idaho, headed towards the Tetons and taken up their search for Jim Allen. All they knew was that he was waiting for his twin brother, Jack Allen, somewhere in the north-western part of Wyoming.

The following morning the sun was shining bright and warm and the whole earth steamed as the two began to wind in, and rise among, the first slopes of the foothills towards the serried peaks of the Tetons.

A short time after their midday halt, Dutchy turned from the smooth trail he had been following, up a long, smooth slant of rock which led to a little side canyon. As they traversed this, it became so steep and rough that they were forced to lead their ponies. As Dutchy reached the top of a stiff, scrambling climb, he turned to the panting Toothpick and grunted:

"Folks calls this here Horse Thief Pass." As he swung on his pony, he added: "She splits here so we'd better scatter. An' if you wants, you can sing high an' handsome."

With that he swung along the right fork. Toothpick gulped the thin air for a moment, climbed into his saddle and struck out along the left fork. As he rode, he lifted his raucous voice in a mournful song.

The tall, long-legged cow-puncher was in an evil mood when he rejoined his companion where the trail flattened out again along another broad shelf.

"Hoss Thief Trail," he grumbled as he squatted on his heels and rolled a cigarette. "I'm bettin' no honest man ever comes this way."

"How come you knows it, Toothpick?" a voice called.

With startled oaths the two men swung about and dropped hands to the butts of their Colts. They stared at the man who had hailed them from the top of a nearby rock; then, as their eyes discerned the features that were concealed behind the scrubby beard that covered his freckled face, they grinned foolishly and hastened forward to meet him.

The man who dropped from the rock and came forward to meet them had the stature of a thin, undersized boy. His clothes were nondescript and worn, his broad-brimmed hat was battered, his face

127

unshaven, he wore moccasins in place of boots, and his feet were unadorned by spurs.

He seemed out of place in this wild country; as though he were more used to riding freight cars than a horse. But there was something in the way his two low-hung guns clung to his slender legs, something in his easy movements, in his alert air, that gave the lie to the first impression and marked him as a man of the ranges rather than a hobo. His face was split in a wide, loose grin as he shook hands with them.

"When I hears Toothpick warblin', I figgers I'm havin' a nightmare. How come you drifted up here?" he asked pointedly.

"We was huntin' you —" Dutchy began.

Toothpick broke in: "An' we knows you was aimin' to meet your brother Jack, hereabouts, an' when a letter comes for you from eastern Wyomin', care of me an' marked forward, we figgers it's perhaps from Jack, so we brings it along."

At the look of astonishment on Jim Allen's face, Toothpick hastened to add:

"I has the itchin' foot an' aims to see this country, anyhow."

"An' my folks live in the Wind River country," Dutchy explained.

"You're both darned liars — you come way up here just to bring me a letter!" Then, as Allen accepted the rumpled and dirty letter, he looked up at Dutchy and asked slyly: "You was born hereabouts. Is that how you come to know the Horse Thief Trail?"

Dutchy looked embarrassed, then grinned.

"Well, you see, I was sure wild an' free when I was a kid."

Allen tore open the envelope, wrinkled his brow in thought, and slowly read the few written lines.

"He says his hoss fell on him an' broke his leg an' for me to go home to the Painted Desert an' he'll come visit me next year after he cleans up some hoss thieves for the United Stage & Freight Company."

"They has their lines over in the Big Horn country," Dutchy volunteered.

"Too bad about Jack," Toothpick commented.

"Too bad nothin'! When he gets this leg well, I hopes he gets tother one busted. Jack ain't got no sense a-tall, an' he'll live a heap longer if he's safe in bed with a busted leg," Allen grumbled; then continued: "He's so reckless he don't think nothin' a-tall about tacklin' a bunch of hoss thieves all by his lonesome. No, sir, he ain't got no sense a-tall!"

Toothpick and Dutchy grinned as they recalled the scene three weeks ago at Silent's gambling house.

Allen turned and led the way up a shelving bank to where he had pitched his camp in a gap in the canyon's wall. A gaunt grey horse trotted forward to meet him, nosed in his pockets, and, finding nothing there, reared and snapped her teeth like castanets. Swearing affectionately at the mare, he turned and glanced around for a moment. His face was old, and his smile twisted as he said:

"I keep forgettin' Queen is dead an' keep lookin' for her. That ole hoss an' me sure travelled some. We sure did a lot of wanderin'!" He hesitated a moment, then

129

grinned the old lovable grin his listeners knew so well. But his eyes were moist as he continued: "Yeh, I sure thought a lot of Queen, an' you know her filly, the Princess here, keeps tryin' to back-track to find her. She sure was a hoss an' she sure made one fine last run!"

There was silence for a moment as Allen pottered with the mixing of some flapjacks.

"Where's Jack laid up at?" Dutchy asked.

"At the 7 Bar 7 Ranch on the Crawlin' Stone Creek."

"Huh, ole man Watson's place," Dutchy explained: "Salt River country. 'Tain't more than a hundred miles from here."

"I'd sure like to see Jack; I ain't seen him for nigh on two years," Allen said wistfully. "An' he's got Honey Boy — the only son Queen ever had."

"I'll show you the trail."

" 'Tain't safe to travel with me."

"Huh, I'll take you a way no one'll see us a-tall!"

Allen looked up with a sudden grin and the other two sighed their relief when they saw his eyes were once more clear. "Jack's so darned conshenshus with his sheriffin' an' special marshallin' that maybe he'll arrest me — think it's his duty. But I'm sure goin' to see him!"

Noon of the following day found the three resting in a small, cuplike depression on the rim of the divide. About them mountain peaks, sharp at their bare summits like teeth, holding fields of snow lower down, thrust upwards towards the cloudless blue dome of the heavens. They had finished their cold flapjacks and

130

bacon when Dutchy, followed by the others, made his way through the tall pines to the edge of an abrupt cliff.

"See them lakes down there an' them green patches?" he asked as he pointed. "That's Jackson's Hole."

"I've heard tell of it as where gents —" Toothpick interrupted himself and glanced hastily towards Jim-twin Allen.

"Gents like me, who is wanted bad, can hide out." Allen finished Toothpick's sentence with a cheerful grin.

Steep ranges, sheer walls of canyons closed it in on every side, and each entrance lay through intricate mountain trails. Snake River entered it through a sheer-walled canyon and went out through a deep chasm at the other end.

Many crooked paths vanished in that famous sanctuary. Law stopped at its borders, for there was always an open season on sheriffs and marshals down there. It would take a foolhardy sheriff, or one with a heavily armed posse, to dare enter one of its almost impregnable, secret trails.

Towards sundown they were picking a difficult way along the banks of a twisting creek that flowed between high, rocky walls. Just where this opened into the canyon of the Green River, they cut the trail of many horses heading towards the north and Jackson's Hole.

"Them tracks ain't more than two hours old," Allen commented after studying them for a moment. "They was made since the sun went out of here."

Dutchy nodded.

"Three gents drove 'em."

"Reckon they is some of the hoss thieves Jack aims to get. The dern fool, he ain't got no sense a-tall, figgerin' he can lick a whole county of hoss thieves by his lonesome," Allen said in deep disgust.

Their trail lay along the way where the hoof-prints of the stolen horses were, and they rode silently, each engrossed in his own thoughts. Suddenly there came to their ears the dull boom of several distant rifle shots. Instinctively, they pulled up their ponies and listened.

"Huh, I guess they leaves a couple of gents back a ways to sorta discourage the man who once owned them hosses," Toothpick announced.

Farther on, where the canyon walls closed in, and the trail grew narrow and steep, the clink of an iron-shod hoof against rock warned them of the approach of a fast-travelling horse. Then just as the trail angled sharply to the right, a horse and rider wheeled suddenly around the turn and his mount slid to a stiff-legged halt. Caught by surprise, the man sat and stared for a moment.

Dutchy was leading and Allen trailing and it was the former who broke the stillness by the laconic greeting:

"Howdy!"

The rider grunted in reply. Then, as Dutchy moved over to allow him to pass, he urged his pony forward with his hand hovering close to his pistol butt and slowly commenced to edge past them. He had passed Toothpick and was abreast of Allen. It was almost dark and for the first time the unknown rider clearly saw the

132

latter's face. For the space of an eye-wink the man stared; then, as his gun came free, he cried:

"Allen!"

There came the spurt of flame and the echoing roar of Allen's heavy Colt as he fired from his hip. The man rocked in his saddle, his gun clattered to the ground, and he leaned forward and grasped the horn of his saddle. His horse reared and went clattering off down the trail. Like a flash, Allen swung his grey about and started in pursuit. Before they had gone fifty feet, Princess was abreast of the other pony, Allen leaned forward, seized the man by the arm, and sent him tumbling to the ground.

"I was sure scared when I sees that gent dig for his gun," Toothpick whispered to Dutchy as the two rode back towards Allen.

"Me, too!" Dutchy responded. "But he's like a snake — quick! You can't never surprise him. You could step on him when he's asleep an' git bit sure."

It was Jim-twin Allen's perfect co-ordination between mind and muscles, as well as an animal-like instinct, that made it almost impossible to get him at a disadvantage, and wrote his name in the Book of Time as the best, or the worst, of all the outlaws and gunmen of the old West.

"Know him?" Allen asked as Dutchy swung from his pony.

Turning the man over on his back, Dutchy lit a match, stooped, and carefully examined the mudstained face. Then he grunted:

"Yeh, I knows him. 'Snake' Wilson — a no-good breed killer."

The man's eyes fluttered open. He painfully raised himself on his elbow, groped with his right hand at his empty holster, glared up at Allen and snarled:

"You yellow houn'! I bet you would never dare show your ugly mug in Basin, 'cause I knows you was scared of 'Bull' — an' I wins two hundred cartwheels. Broken leg!" he exclaimed in sarcasm; then choked and gagged. With a desperate effort, the man aroused himself. "You come sneakin' in the back way an' you had your gun on me all the time."

With that he fell back in a shapeless huddle of sprawling limbs. He twitched a moment, then lay still.

"He knew you," Dutchy said.

"Not any," Toothpick corrected. "Snake thinks Jim here is his brother Jack."

Allen thoughtfully rubbed the month's stubble on his chin, looked up at his two tall companions, and grinned. "Jack is a prideful cuss an' goes in for whiskers. Figgers they makes him look more like a man than a peanut."

"This Snake person sure makes a bad mistake goin' off half cocked. Though if you had been Jack, he'd have got you when he went so unexpected like for his gun."

But Allen disdained Toothpick's eulogy.

"Nope; Jack is faster than me and all around a better man."

While both Dutchy and Toothpick doubted this statement, they knew of Allen's intense admiration for his brother and decided to leave it uncontradicted.

134

"Humans is sure funny," Toothpick philosophised. "Snake was prideful about winnin' two hundred cartwheels an' him travellin' to hell fast."

"I forgets that!" Allen spoke sharply. "He bets Jack is scared to go to Basin an' face a gent named Bull —"

"Kinda looks as if folks hereabouts thought Jack's busted leg warn't real, an' was a bum excuse for not showin' up in Basin," Toothpick drawled.

Allen stood for a moment in thought, then said:

"This Snake person makes two mistakes. He thinks he won that there bet he made about Jack not goin' to Basin. But he ain't. 'Cause if Jack can't go, I'll let these here whiskers keep growin' an' go talk to Mr. Bull myself."

After the three had mounted their horses and, leaving Snake Wilson sprawling on the trail, were picking their way down the darkened canyon, Toothpick leaned over and whispered to Dutchy:

"I'm feelin' sorry for this here Mr. Bull, an' I'm aimin' to head for this town of Basin."

CHAPTER
SIXTEEN

The New Sheriff

There are many such towns as Basin dotting the West from the frontier of Canada to the Mexican border. Each is like the other, a group of dust-covered houses dropped aimlessly into the wilderness. A long, wide street littered with old bottles and tin cans, knee-deep in dust during summer and a veritable quagmire of clinging mud during the rainy season, a couple of stores, a freight and stage station, an hotel, two eating houses, ten saloons and one church — such is Basin.

Just as a rider followed by a pack horse came from the south and passed the outskirts of the town, the sun caught with its long, slanting rays the piles of tin cans and broken bottles thrown out from the saloons and turned them into mammoth, glittering diamonds.

Jauntily, head back, sitting very straight in his saddle, one hand caressing his moustache or pulling his silky beard, looking neither to the right nor the left, the rider moved slowly down the centre of the street to the northern end of town.

His hat, with its extra high crown, was the finest grade of Stetson; his boots — custom-turned patent leather — had abnormally high heels; his shirt was of silk, his bandanna a bright scarlet, his clothes were black and silk-faced lapels adorned his long-tailed coat.

A tall, long-legged, gawky cow-puncher, who was sitting in a rocker on the porch of the Basin House, spat out a toothpick and whispered to his companion excitedly:

"Dutchy, it's him!"

"Yep! But I wouldn't have knowed him but for his horse."

"Ain't he the hellion?" Toothpick asked joyfully. "He stole his Brother Jack's clothes."

"An' his hoss!" Dutchy grinned as he nodded towards the grey pack horse.

"He sure did," chuckled the gawky cow-puncher as he threw away another chewed toothpick. "That's Honey Boy for certain."

Toothpick unhooked his long legs from the railing, scrambled to his feet and stepped from the porch on to the street. But the rider passed him with no sign of recognition and continued up the street to the offices of the United Stage & Freight Company.

There he swung from the saddle and strutted into the office. Before a counter three clerks were scratching busily in ledgers, and behind them several teamsters swapped yarns. The man swung about and headed directly towards a door marked:

E. A. Hines,
General Manager, Private.

"Hey, fellow, what do you want? You can't go in there. Can't you read?" a clerk blustered as the stranger approached the door.

But the man was evidently deaf, blind, or did not believe in signs, for he ignored the outraged clerk, shoved the door open, passed through and shut it behind him; then he turned to face the two men who looked up in surprise as he entered.

"Which of you gents is Mr. Hines?"

A thin, bald-headed, emaciated man of fifty, sitting before a roll-top desk, hesitated for a moment, glanced at his companion and said:

"That's me."

"I'm Jack-twin Allen."

As he stated his name, he caught a flicker of surprise and of something else — something that seemed like fear in the second man's bulging grey eyes.

"I'm right glad to meet you!" Hines spoke cordially. "I — we — were beginning to fear you would be unable to come."

"Unable — or afraid!" The man with the grey eyes laughed loudly.

Allen turned and looked directly at the speaker, who, when he caught the yellow flare in those strangely shaped eyes, felt little prickles of fear chase themselves up and down his spine. After a few seconds Allen spoke softly:

"You knows now you was mistaken."

Here Hines hastened to say:

"Mr. Allen, meet Mr. Boomer, owner of the hotel and one of the town committee men."

138

Boomer mopped his round, red face with a handkerchief, rose to his feet and thrust out a hand as he cried heartily:

"Pleased to meet you, Jack."

Allen ignored the hand and explained:

"I never shakes hands with nobody."

Boomer was a tall, powerfully built man who could have crushed Allen with ease in a hand-to-hand struggle. He cultivated a hearty, jovial manner and, nodding his head, he grinned broadly and said:

"That's all right, my friend, I understand. You dassent take no chances."

But he had struck a slightly false note in these remarks. He was too cordial — too quick to claim a friend.

"You're wrong twice. I always take chances an' I'm not your friend." Then, turning to Hines, Allen continued: "As I understands it, you sent for me to catch horse thieves, an' you're goin' to make me sheriff, 'cause you wants it done legal."

"Mr. Boomer and I form a majority of the committee men. I have your papers all made out, so I will first hand them and your star to you; then we can adjourn, have a drink, and explain matters."

With that, Hines yanked open a drawer, took out a folded paper and a star and handed them to Allen, who stuffed the paper in his pocket, carefully pinned the star to his left lapel and looked up with an amused grin. His eyes twinkled as he said:

"I sure likes the looks of that thing."

139

"Not the first you've worn," Boomer chuckled. There was a touch of malice in his voice as he added: "You're the fourth man who has worn it."

"They all dead?" Allen asked unconcernedly.

"We planted two and the other quit."

"Well, I ain't figgerin' on gettin' planted or quittin'," Allen said confidently.

Curiously enough both his listeners believed him, though their reactions were entirely different.

Followed by the other two, Hines led the way to the outer office and said:

"Boys, this is Jack Allen, who is goin' to make your trips easier for you."

They all swung eagerly towards Allen; then, when they noted his gaudy clothes and small stature, their faces grew blank with disappointment. Allen looked at them carefully and then walked towards a broad-shouldered teamster and asked:

"You savvy hosses?"

This was as much a statement as a question, and the teamster stuttered in surprise.

"Yes — yes, sir. I loves hosses."

"Then take my two greys, rub 'em down, feed 'em, an' bed 'em down. An' tend to 'em like they was your mother."

Flustered and flattered at being picked out from his mates by the famous gunman and sheriff, the teamster stuttered that he would attend to them.

As they swung out of the office into the street Allen heard one man cry contemptuously: "Bull will have his scalp afore the week is up."

140

"It don't take strength to flip a gun," another man insisted, "an' I'm betting all I has that he makes hoss thieves hard to find in the Big Horn."

"Who's Bull?" Allen asked as they reached the hotel.

"Bull —" Hines glanced carefully about before continuing: "Bull Morgan has a ranch over on the Grey Bull River and owns the El Dorado Hall at the far end of town."

"Which tells me nothin'!" Allen grinned. "You suspects he's mixed up with this hoss stealin'?"

"Heaven forbid!" Hines denied hastily. "But there is folks who has that idea."

"But they keeps that idea to themselves when Bull is present," Boomer exclaimed.

They entered the long room of the hotel bar. After they had ordered their drinks, Allen turned to Boomer and asked bluntly:

"This Bull person a friend of yourn?"

Two cow-punchers and the bartender who heard this remark smirked at Boomer's flustered face and glanced curiously at Allen.

"No, Bull ain't no friend of mine," Boomer replied sulkily.

The more he saw of Allen the less he liked him and the more he feared him.

"Why?"

"Nothin'. Only I thought you spoke his name sorta affectionate like."

Raising his glass, Allen caught sight of Toothpick and Dutchy in a far corner of the room. He grinned at them

141

as he touched his star with his glass and tossed down his drink.

"I knows Jack Allen," a loud voice called, "an' I'm bettin' he don't dare come, an' if he does Bull will spank the little runt."

Very slowly, Allen turned and glanced towards the speaker who was staring at a couple of punchers with his hand on his gun.

"Who's that gent?" Allen asked Hines.

"He's a bad character called 'Spike' Sullivan," Hines whispered in warning. "He's treacherous and dangerous."

Allen grinned.

"Reckon now it's time to start sheriffin'."

Strutting slowly like a gamecock, he walked directly towards the bully who closed his hand over his pistol butt.

"You says you know Jack Allen, an' he's yellow?"

The bully stared.

"Mr. Spike Sullivan, tell these here gents you lied!"

The voice was gentle, but it seemed as if somewhere a death knell was tolling, and silence, like magic, fell on the large room.

Spike Sullivan's face grew hard and his eyes contemptuous, but when he sighted the black hole of Allen's Colt and the yellow wolf-like eyes behind the gun, his manner changed. He stood motionless for a moment, and then growled:

"You got the drop on me."

"Not now!" With a smooth motion, Allen dropped his Colt back into its holster and demanded: "Tell these here gents you lied!"

142

Visibly to the watchers' eyes the bully's courage oozed away, his hand fell limply from the butt of his gun, and he choked and stammered. At length he spoke hesitatingly:

"I never see Jack Allen!"

"That'll be enough," Allen said gently. "Now you go tell Bull Morgan, if he's curious he can come civil-like an' ask my name, or he can come a-runnin' with a gun in his hand."

Murderous with baffled rage, the bully spun about and almost ran from the room.

Allen walked towards Toothpick and Dutchy.

"You two darn fools followin' me about is aimin' to get yourselves killed."

Dutchy hitched up his belt and shrugged.

"Not any. We figgered we might come in sorta handy."

Toothpick's face was cut by a broad grin, and his blue eyes were snapping with excitement.

"You got a job for us?"

"Yeh; tendin' jail!" Allen grinned at Toothpick's crestfallen face.

"Herdin' prisoners?"

"Yeh; an' no lynchin's, nor —" Allen commenced.

"Nor no rescues," Toothpick interrupted and added with satisfaction: "An' I figgers there will be plenty of both. I takes the job."

"The jail is opposite the stage offices. You go down there an' I'll be there right pronto."

The two nodded, trailed their spurs across the floor, and vanished through the door. Allen returned to Hines.

143

"I wants two deputies to guard the jail. Does I get 'em?"

"A dozen if you want them."

"Two is enough." Allen thought a moment, and then asked: "I hears you have plenty of killin's in town?"

"Yep," the interested bartender broke in, "we has plenty."

"You pass the word around quiet-like that from now on they don't go. Any gent what draws steel goes to the calaboose."

The bartender nodded and thoughtfully studied Allen, who turned to Hines.

"Let's go see the jail."

After they had left, the bartender rubbed his bald head thoughtfully for a moment; then addressing the two cow-punchers and Boomer he asked surprisedly:

"Any of you gents ever in Kansas?"

One of the cow-punchers nodded.

"You knows how a cyclone starts — a little harmless-lookin' black cloud in the sky? An' then it gets bigger an' cleans things up proper an' then fades away. Well, that's what this here Jack Allen reminds me of."

The cow-puncher spoke thoughtfully:

"Yeh, I reckons it's time for certain gents to hunt cyclone holes."

His companion pulled out his gun, regarded it critically for a moment, and grinned.

"An' I figgers the time's comin' — pronto — when a gent what packs a gun will be called ostentatious, like a gent what wears spurs in an office."

144

Boomer gulped two hasty drinks. His forehead was lined with deep wrinkles of thought. Then he hastened across the street, entered a small saloon, crossed to a cow-puncher and whispered:

"Get your horse an' hit the breeze. Tell Bull to come quick, 'cause hell is sure goin' to break loose."

CHAPTER
SEVENTEEN

An Invitation Refused

The jail was well and strongly built, and was brand new. It had been built largely by money furnished by the United Stage & Freight Company, who had determined to have a jail which would hold any horse thief they were lucky enough to catch.

In the front a grilled door led to the street. Doors opened from the hall to the office, and on the opposite side of the corridor, to a pair of bedrooms and a kitchen. At the end of the hall another barred door led into a passage containing eight cells, four on either side.

"Huh!" Allen said thoughtfully after he, Dutchy and Toothpick had been shown about by Hines. "She's sure built solid. Better'n any I've ever been in."

Toothpick snorted, but quelled his mirth at a glance from Allen.

They found a short, stocky, jovial-faced cattleman awaiting them when they returned to the office after their inspection of the jail.

"This is Mr. 'Chuck' Newson, the third committee man," Hines introduced.

"I'm powerful glad to meet you, Mr. Allen," Newson said enthusiastically. "This country ain't safe for an honest man no more. Bull Morgan has a strangle-hold on the county, an' it needs a sure enough man to break it loose."

Allen rose briskly to his feet.

"We'll talk medicine later," he said. Then he questioned: "Gents have been bettin' free an' easy that Jack Allen dassent show in town?"

The two committee men nodded.

"Then I figger I better walk about — show myself — an' sorta lay down the law."

"Mrs. Newson sent me special to ask you to eat with us tonight. It's all ready, so let's eat, an' we'll talk things over later. She got a barrel of apples from her home town in Vermont, an' has two of the darnedest pies baked you ever saw."

Allen's face broke into a wide grin, and the two committee men chuckled inwardly at the greedy look in his eyes. Then his face clouded and he hesitated.

"You say she's got fresh apple pie?"

"You bet you! An' the crust just melts in your mouth."

Allen's inward struggle with his greed was apparent to all. After a time he shook his head and said regretfully:

"I reckon I can't. You gents feed, then meet me back here. I'm goin' to look around. Toothpick, you come with me."

Later, when they were walking down the darkened street, Toothpick asked curiously:

"How come you refuse that invite?"

147

"Do you think Mrs. Newson would invite The Wolf to eat her pie?" Allen queried.

"But —"

"There ain't no buts!" Allen spoke sadly. "It don't make no difference to a hoss thief who he gets downed by. So that's all fair. But I ain't aimin' to mix socially with decent folks an' ladies who would sure drop dead with fright if they knowed I was the Killer Wolf an' not the sheriff, Jack Allen."

Toothpick remained silent. He knew, as few other men knew, that Jim Allen's outlawry had been committed largely to right wrongs. Allen was a sort of vigilance committee of one. Yet, nevertheless, people who did not know The Wolf feared him.

"You go in the Chink restaurant and rustle some grub. An' see if the darned heathen has any pie. I'll see you back at the jail later."

"Me, I'm comin' with you!" Toothpick stated firmly.

"Nope; my play's stronger if I does it alone."

As Basin was a typical frontier town, so also was the El Dorado Saloon typical of its kind. A long bar on one side of the room, glittering bottles and stacked glasses, two badly done oil paintings and a mounted elk's head completed its adornments. A shirt-sleeved, white-aproned bartender mopped the bar, and gossiped with the customers.

At the rear, folding doors led into a hall with several tables. At one of these, a fat, bald-headed man, with a battered, rimless derby perched on his head, slipped cards from the bottom of the deck while several men opposite him covered the exposed cards with stacks of silver coins. Monte was for pikers; those who had more money played faro at a table on the other side of the room.

The El Dorado was doing a land-office business. Men leaned against the bar and drank, or else milled about the floor discussing the unexpected arrival of Jack Allen.

"I'm bettin' he dassent come here," a thin, gawky man said tauntingly.

A slender, thin-lipped, hard-faced man swung about and asked:

"You're bettin'? How much?"

The gawky man slammed several gold pieces down on the bar and chortled.

"I'm bettin' all I has that Jack Allen dassent show up here tonight!"

The slender man covered the money and drawled:

"Folks calls me 'Kansas' Jones. I never seen Jack Allen, but if he's got half the sand of that little runt, the money's mine."

With that he pointed to a Wanted notice pasted on the mirror behind the bar. Beneath the heavily typed "Dead or Alive", an ageless, wolf-like, ruthless pictured face was above the name "Jim-twin Allen".

"I seen that little runt walk into Big Rock an' clean out a bunch of better gunslingers than Bull has!"

Suddenly a thick, heavy silence fell upon the room. Everyone turned as the swinging doors opened, and Allen stepped in. He stood there for a moment, glancing coolly about him; then, with his coat tails

149

flapping, his chin held high and his high-heeled boots tapping sharply on the floor, he stalked forward.

"Gents, I'm Jack Allen, the new sheriff!" He grinned cheerfully into the staring, expectant faces. "I'm plumb sorry for the gents what lost money on my not showin'."

Several of them grinned, but almost everyone stared with hostile, cold eyes. Allen ignored their enmity and said with a cheerful indifference:

"Bartender, I'm buyin' said gents a drink. Set 'em up."

No one moved; no one accepted the consolation drink. There was a chilly silence for a long moment. Then Kansas Jones stepped forward, jingled the money he had just won from the thin, gawky man, glanced about and said with a sneer:

"Reckon there ain't no gents what lost money present. Which is plumb strange, 'cause I won some, which I'm now buyin' you a drink with."

A low buzz of conversation began. The bartender slid out two glasses and Allen and Kansas solemnly drank.

"Here's how!"

Then Allen invited Kansas to have another, and after that was downed he turned to the barkeeper, raised his voice slightly, and said:

"I ain't worryin' none about what happened yesterday. But I'm tellin' you to pass the news that I won't stand no killin's nor no crooked gamblers about town."

Suddenly his face changed, and his eyes flared yellow as he caught sight of the thin, gawky man's face in the

150

mirror. Allen swung towards him and said in such a soft voice that no one heard him:

"You're 'Chalk-eye' Kent, from down New Mex way. You're a no-good killer. There ain't no place for you in this town. Get out before sunup!"

In the same way as Spike Sullivan's courage had oozed away from him earlier that evening, now Chalk-eye's slipped from him as he met those flaring, yellow eyes. He mumbled something, then turned and walked with an exaggerated swagger out of the saloon.

After Allen had left the crowd swayed forward and began discussing the little sheriff.

"Bull will eat him up," one of them sneered.

"He's got nerve," another allowed.

"An' I didn't see any of you gents gettin' personal when he was present," Kansas taunted.

Then an angry, shrill voice from the back room stilled the clamour. A silence for a moment; then —

"I saw you cheat. The game's crooked!"

Another silence. Then the boom of a heavy Colt.

People crowded into the rear room and, after a moment, came straggling back again.

"Johnson downed that pilgrim kid," someone informed the bartender.

"Darn shame. The kid warn't heeled, neither," someone else accused.

"That calls your bluff, Mr. Jack Allen," the barman chuckled as he polished a glass. "Let's see if you can run Johnson outa his own place for downin' that there kid!"

151

Back at the jail, Jim Allen was looking with disgust at the pie Toothpick had brought from the Chinese restaurant.

"You calls that pie?" He picked it up and let it fall back to the plate with a dull thud. "Well, I s'pose I got to eat it."

"That other grey you got — that's Honey Boy, Jack's hoss?" Toothpick queried.

"Yeh! I kinda borrowed him. He's the only son Queen ever had. Jack is sure due to skin me alive. I give it to him a coupla years ago. Sorta sorry I did now, 'cause I's used to havin' two hosses follow me aroun'."

"Does he eat pie like Princess does?"

"Sure. I trained him before I give him to Jack."

Then the little gunman explained how he had gone to see his brother Jack, whom he found in bed with a fractured leg. Jack had fumed with helpless rage at the reports that he was afraid to come to Basin. So Jim had quietly appropriated Jack's boots, clothes and horse and had come in his place.

"How you aimin' to fix Bull?"

"I'll just wait aroun' an' sorta nag him into committin' an overt act."

Then Allen went out to feed the remains of the pie to his pets while Toothpick diligently searched the dictionary for the word "overt", which he meant to add to his own vocabulary.

A short time later two very excited committee men appeared and asked for Allen.

"He's over to the stable feedin' his hosses pie," Toothpick informed them with a grin.

"That's fine," Hines said. "We were afraid he had went to the El Dorado to arrest Johnson."

"Why for?"

They explained how Johnson had killed an unarmed boy at the El Dorado that evening, and they were afraid that Allen would go and attempt to carry out his threat to arrest the first man who drew a gun in Basin.

"We are in time now to stop him." Chuck Newson sighed his relief.

"You think you is!" Toothpick ejaculated.

Then all three turned to face Allen, who strutted into the room. Rapidly the two committee men, both talking at the same time, explained how impossible it was for Allen to think of arresting the first man who ignored his warning that no gun play went in Basin.

"This Johnson is Bull's partner?" Allen asked.

They nodded.

Allen grinned at Toothpick.

"Then I reckon it's time to start makin' Bull commit that overt act!"

"The place is filled with Bull's men!" Hines protested.

"You gents wait here. I'll be back pronto with a pris'ner."

After Allen had left Hines asked Toothpick anxiously:

"Surely he won't attempt to take Johnson out of the El Dorado?"

"Don't you worry none!" Toothpick smiled confidently; but inwardly he felt none of the confidence his words implied. "The fool little runt will sure get dropped some day!" he growled to himself.

CHAPTER
EIGHTEEN

First Prisoner

In the early days in the cattle country rustling did not have the sinister meaning it acquired later. A rustler was a cowboy who hunted maverick calves either for himself or his employer. If for the latter, he received five dollars a head. Thus it was easy for an ambitious cowboy to make legally considerably more than his salary.

But when the big ranchers — many of them Eastern men who never saw a cow — joined together and formed the Cattle Association, it was decreed that a cowboy would no longer be allowed to rustle mavericks for himself, but must mark each one found with his employer's brand, and that he would receive no extra pay for this.

The cow-punchers and small owners were quick to resent this rule. Hence the rustler who still plied his trade and branded mavericks had the sympathy of everyone, excepting the members of the Cattle Association.

Then the cow-puncher began branding not only mavericks but other calves which even the unwritten law gave him no right to; but still public opinion was with him, for the calves so branded belonged in most

154

cases to Eastern outsiders whom the residents of the West resented for their greater wealth.

The men of the mountains, outlaws and killers, were quick to take advantage of this situation and poured into the cattle country to make some easy money. Little by little a loose organisation sprang up among rustlers, and it needed only a strong man to knit it firmly together.

Such a man was Bull Morgan. Big, powerful, brainy, with a tremendous personality, he soon had the cattle barons fighting hard for their lives. He and his chosen band confined themselves to running off horses. In a country where the horse was the only means of travel, it had the value of several cows. He cleverly kept the sympathy of the majority of the people by aiding them occasionally when they were rustling cows from the cattle barons. But Bull had one failing: he was too grasping. He couldn't play straight.

Soon his men, recruited from the worst class of outlaws, began to sweep in horses belonging to the smaller ranchers. Suddenly the county awoke to the fact that they were helpless, and that they were being robbed by the very gang of which they thought they were honorary members. Then also the country became unsafe; people were robbed, women insulted.

Such was the situation when Jim Allen, playing the part of his brother, Jack, became sheriff. If he wanted success, he must separate the sheep from the wolves. If he declared war on all rustlers, the whole country would rise against him. So he decided to wage war on Bull's gang — not as rustlers but as murderers.

He had gathered from the rancher where he had stopped for his noon meal before entering Basin, that the better class of citizens were ready to give up rustling from the big cattle barons in exchange for law and order. For Bull's men had made all married men with wives and families, or men with stock of their own, afraid to leave their ranches for any length of time.

So Jim Allen welcomed the chance to strike at Bull Morgan through his partner, Tom Johnson. Jim knew that if he succeeded in arresting Johnson and took him from a place crowded with Bull's men to the jail, he would be hitting a severe blow to Bull's prestige and force him openly to side with Johnson. This would instantly turn the better class of men against Bull, for the killing that evening had been murder pure and simple.

When Jim-twin Allen walked from the jail he headed direct to the El Dorado Saloon. But before he had covered half the distance he slowed his brisk pace and, a moment later, came to a halt.

"You dern fool!" he told himself. "What do you aim to do? Ain't you got no sense? Can't you remember you're sheriff now, an' got to act like a human an' not like a wolf? Jack, he'd figger out a way to get Johnson outa there alive an' arrest him lawful an' not fill him full of lead!"

Frowning deeply, figuring how the thing could be done legally, Allen made his way to the front of the El Dorado Saloon and peered in. Then slipping like a shadow along the wall, he made his way through the darkness to the rear. Here he discovered a door at

156

the top of two steps. Gently lifting the latch, he opened it a trifle and glanced in.

The door opened into the crowded gambling room. Allen chuckled softly when he noted that the door opened outward; then he closed it gently. He searched about, discovered a heavy plank, placed this close to the wall, then slipped silently through the door and closed it gently behind him.

Tom Johnson was a slender man of medium height with a cold, impassive, hawklike face. Dressed in the long frock coat of his class, he was typical of the professional gambler. To his left sat the marker; behind him, on a high chair, was the look-out. Both were replicas of Johnson; neither had quite such expert hands, for Johnson had the reputation among his cronies of making "the case talk". Both were as coldly unscrupulous as their superior.

A cattle buyer, a big rancher, and several cow-punchers were hitting the sky. It was a big game, and at times large sums of money were on the table. Johnson believed in dealing a square game whenever possible and letting the percentage work for the house. But both the cattle buyer and the rancher were winners, and both had coppered the queen for a large sum; and Johnson knew that the queen was due to lose; so his hands hovered over the case a fraction of a second longer than usual and when the cards slipped out, the queen won instead of losing.

Johnson had been so absorbed in this delicate operation that he failed to note the opening of the back door or the little figure which tiptoed towards him.

157

With cold, impassive eyes he glanced up as he raked in the counters and found the cattle buyer studying him with a speculative eye. Had he bungled? Was the cattleman suspicious? Had he seen enough to be sure of cheating like that fool kid? And if so what would he do? Johnson was debating these questions when a strange voice said softly:

"Johnson, I want you!"

Johnson turned to face the speaker. He noted the guns held in each hand and the star pinned to the lapel of the man's coat.

"Who are you? What do you want me for?"

"I'm Jack Allen, the new sheriff, an' I want you for murdering a kid tonight!"

The gamblers, as well as Johnson, were inclined to laugh at the serious little bewhiskered man who thought he could arrest Bull Morgan's partner in his own place. There were a dozen men who would start firing at a word from their boss. But there was something about Allen that made Johnson pause. For the steady stare in his queer eyes cried a warning, and even if the shiny star did not spell authority, the two guns did.

"Johnson, keep your hands up an' stan' on your legs. An' if one of your men lets out a single yap, I'll drop you an' him!" Softly spoken, the words held a greater menace than if they had been shouted.

The gambler allowed his eyes to stray about the room and then cursed. For the click of coins at the monte table told him that none but his immediate neighbours knew of his predicament. For the players

158

blocked the scene from the others in the room even as he himself offered a perfect screen for Allen in case either the look-out or marker went into action.

"I'm not speakin' again — stand up!" Allen spoke slowly with a pause between each word. As Johnson obeyed, the gun in his lap clattered to the floor.

"Turn your back an' walk slowly backwards!" Then Allen turned to the two other gamblers. "If either one of you makes a break I cashes him!"

Slowly, quietly, the two backed towards the rear door. One gun pressed against Johnson's spine and the other covered the petrified gamblers. As he reached the door, Allen pushed it open, then swung his right gun upward and gave Johnson a smart tap on the jaw. Before he had recovered his wits, Allen had dropped the heavy plank against the door and was prodding Johnson with his gun. To save his spine from being fractured by the gun rapping against it, Johnson was forced to jog trot down the street to the jail.

Pandemonium broke out the moment the door slammed and Allen vanished. The gamblers snatched out their guns and hurled themselves against the door. Seconds passed before they realised it was blocked from the outside. And when they rushed from the front entrance in pursuit, they were too late.

When Jim Allen pushed the door of the town jail open and thrust the scowling Johnson in ahead of him, he was grinning cheerfully, for he had won the first trick. Bull would be forced to aid his partner, and the moment he did so he would lose the sympathy of the class of men whom Allen was trying to get on his side.

159

The little group — Boomer, Newson, Hines, Dutchy and Toothpick — who were awaiting him, jumped to their feet and pushed forward to meet him.

"You got him!" Hines cried in blank amazement.

"Tol' you he allus gets what he goes after!" Toothpick chuckled.

Boomer's hearty manner fell away from him like a mask and he sneered.

"Now you got him, what you goin' to do with him?"

Allen grinned easily.

"Lock him up an' keep him safe for the hangman!"

"I'll be out on bail tomorrow, an' then you hunt your hole!" Johnson snarled.

None too gently, Dutchy and Toothpick searched the furious prisoner, and after relieving him of everything but his socks, shirt and pants, thrust him out of the door towards the cell block. Grinning broadly, Toothpick opened the door of one of the cells, shoved Johnson in, locked it securely, and said:

"Breakfast is at seven. Don't you be late or we won't keep it for you."

Then ignoring the other's murderous look and jingling the keys happily, he returned to the office. As he entered Allen spoke thoughtfully:

"You figger Judge Handler will turn Johnson loose?"

"The minute he strikes town," Boomer snapped. "So your spectacular play means nothin'. We want you to catch horse thieves, not —"

"When's the judge due back?" Allen asked Hines.

"Tomorrow."

"What does he do besides judgin'?"

"Raises hosses over on Gooseberry Creek," Hines explained. "All pure stock."

"An' he takes care of Bull's friends in exchange for leavin' his stock alone?" Allen asked bluntly. From the silence which followed this remark he knew he had hit on the truth. "How many men is I allowed?" Allen asked after a moment's thought.

"You have two now. That's all the town will pay for!" Boomer snapped.

"My company will pay for as many as you want," Hines broke in quickly.

"You bet you!" Newson interjected. "You can have all you want."

Allen turned to Hines. "Mr. Hines, I'd like to speak to you private-like."

Taking the hint, Boomer and Newson unwillingly departed.

The moment the door clanged shut, Allen turned to Dutchy and asked:

"You know six men what can handle a rifle an' will do what they're told?"

"Yeh; my dad an' my brothers." Dutchy grinned.

Rapidly Allen outlined his plan, and as he did so, Toothpick and Dutchy smiled broadly, and Hines heaved a sigh of relief, for here was a man who had both the brains and nerve to free the country of Bull Morgan's strangle grip.

"I'll be goin' with you, Dutchy, while you gets your horse."

As Dutchy was saddling his pony, Allen spoke regretfully.

161

"This sheriffin' has its drawbacks, 'cause you got to do ever'thin' lawful. It is a darn shame Bull don't go stealin' the judge's hosses. I'm bettin' if some hombre run off a few, the judge wouldn't be lettin' Johnson go free!

"Sheriffin' to hell! Now, if I warn't the sheriff," Allen continued quizzically, "I'd tell you to borrow some of the judge's hosses just to make him mad!"

"An' I knows a place you could hold two hundred head an' the whole country couldn't find them!" Dutchy remarked.

"Well, so-long," Allen called as Dutchy swung his horse and galloped away.

Later that night, as Allen and Toothpick were preparing for bed, the little gunman looked up as he pulled off his boots and said:

"It seems funny walkin' aroun' an' not watchin' for some homicidious sheriff that's on the warpath. Yep, it's sure nice to feel safe!"

Long after Allen's breathing announced he was asleep, Toothpick stared into the darkness and considered this last remark. That night Allen had declared war on a desperate and dangerous gang of horse thieves and yet talked of feeling "safe".

More clearly than words this told Toothpick of the load of danger Allen was forever carrying with him!

CHAPTER
NINETEEN

An Offer

Bull Morgan, big, arrogant, overflowing with confidence, arrived in Basin the following morning about ten. He went directly to the Basin Hotel where he always had a room reserved for him. He nodded to Gus Williams, a furtive-eyed old man who acted as clerk during the early morning hours.

"Tell Boomer and Kansas Jones I want to see them — and send me up something to eat," Bull ordered shortly; then mounted the stairway to a large room that faced on the street.

He had finished his breakfast and was impatiently chewing his second cigar when Boomer and Kansas arrived. The former was nervously self-important, the latter coldly dangerous.

"Glad to see you, Bull," Boomer greeted. "We got to do somethin' about this Jack Allen."

"We?" Bull spoke contemptuously. "Why did you let him get out of the El Dorado last night?"

Boomer stammered; all his importance vanished.

"I — I didn't think he'd go after Johnson."

"I mean the first time. Why didn't you have someone drop him when he first came to the El Dorado? You could have guessed he would come. He's got a rep now, an' if we bushwhack him, folks will do a hell of a lot of talkin'. You botched things. So it's up to you to get a gent with nerve enough to drop him in a fair fight."

Boomer didn't like this, but he was a coward and afraid of Bull, so he turned hopefully towards Kansas and asked:

"Have you nerve enough?"

Before Kansas could reply Bull cut in:

"There's five hundred in it for you."

"Five hundred!" Boomer groaned, for he knew Bull would force him to pay. "That's a lot of money!"

"But not enough for me to drop Jack-twin Allen public!" Kansas said coolly.

Boomer turned to Bull:

"Tell him he'll have to do it or leave town."

Kansas was typical of a certain class of gunmen who would acknowledge no one boss excepting someone he considered faster than himself. He would accept pay to kill but never an order. So now, as he turned towards Boomer, his eyes were mere slits.

Boomer knew that Kansas would never dare draw on him in the presence of Bull, but there was something about the killer's thin mouth that made him wish he had remained silent.

"Boomer, go sit down," Bull ordered. "Kansas, Boomer will make it a thousand if you drop Jack Allen!"

Boomer groaned.

Kansas spoke seriously.

"I ain't takin' no chance!"

164

"Why?" Bull demanded.

"'Cause I don't want no Wolf on my trail!"

"Meanin'?"

"Jim-twin Allen, Jack's brother." Kansas inhaled a deep breath and continued: "That's the gent they call The Wolf along the border. If I downs Jack, Jim would start quick after me, an' the world ain't big enough to stop him ketchin' me some day!"

"You scared of Jim Allen?"

"Just the same as I'm scared of death. They is one and the same thing!"

Bull knew the man before him, and knew that the very fact that he admitted his fear was a proof of his courage. All men are afraid of something, and only men with nerve will admit it. But this made Bull's problem the harder. He would have to find some other man willing to take a chance. He knew how the minds of Western men worked, and realised that if he had Jack Allen assassinated all the better-class citizens would turn against him.

"Won't the judge turn Johnson loose?" Kansas drawled.

"Yeh!" Bull replied and suddenly smiled. "I get you. Johnson is sure hoppin' mad, an' he swings a fast gun."

"Sure!" Boomer smiled with relief. "Get him loose an' he'll do it for nothin'."

"I'm goin' to see the judge now." Bull sprang to his feet, jammed on his hat, and swaggered through the door. Boomer followed him closely. He had no intention of being left alone with Kansas for even a minute.

The judge had just returned from a visit to his ranch on Gooseberry Creek, and Bull found him busily washing the dust of the long trip from his face and hands.

"Mornin', Judge," Bull greeted.

"Howdy," the judge replied after he had wiped his face dry. "What's this I hear about Jack Allen coming to town?"

"That's what I come to see you about," Bull said easily. "He's takin' money from the Cattle Association an' says he's goin' to stop all rustlin'."

"A pretty big job!" The judge smiled. "He'll have to arrest most of the men in this county if he aims to do that!"

"He's smart." Bull considered for a moment, then continued: "He knows I sorta help the little fellows, so he's started to hit at me."

"How?"

"Last night he arrests Johnson, just because he's my partner."

"Well, that proves he has nerve," the judge said. "What excuse did he give?"

"Why, yesterday a young kid gets drunk an' pulls on Johnson an' he has to drop him," Bull explained. "Boomer saw it, an' he says Johnson took a hell of a chance not droppin' the kid before he did — let him get his gun clear out before Johnson went for him."

The judge frowned.

"You know, Bull, there's been too many killings in this town lately. Now I'm willing to turn any of your men loose that are caught rustling, for that is what the people elected me to do —"

"But Allen didn't arrest Johnson for dropping that drunk, but because he's my partner. An' Allen is workin' for the Cattle Association," Bull insisted.

"H'm!" The judge considered. "I can't turn Johnson loose, but I'll free him on bail."

Bull had to rest content with this, but as he walked down the street, he was anything but contented in his mind. He fully realised that the sentiment of the county was turning against him. He was heavily involved in some land speculations, and he needed another three months. At the end of that time he would be ready to throw his force on the side of law and order. He wanted three months, and he began to fear that Jack Allen might prevent him from having it.

Bull found Toothpick alone in the jail for, earlier that morning, Allen had ridden out of town with Hines. Toothpick had his instructions and the moment Bull presented the judge's order, he promptly turned Johnson loose.

Back in El Dorado, Johnson announced to all the world that if Jack Allen were man enough to walk down the street at a given time, he, Johnson, would fill him full of lead.

"Folks say he's fast," Bull cautioned aloud while he inwardly chuckled with satisfaction.

"He'll have to be!" Johnson said grimly as he stalked to his room at the back of the El Dorado.

Bull bit off the end of a cigar and meditated. If Johnson failed to eliminate Allen, he had another plan to relieve the sheriff of his star. For if either Hines or Chuck Newson should resign — or die — it might be possible to have a committee man appointed in their place who would be friendly. A dangerous game, but Bull's need was pressing.

An hour later, Johnson, immaculate in fresh white linen, reappeared, passed Bull with a nod, and proceeded to search the town for Jack Allen.

But one day — two days — a week passed and still Allen did not reappear. Then on the morning of the seventh day, a dust-covered cow-puncher sprang off his wind-blown horse before the judge's office and knocked furiously at the door.

Five minutes later the judge stormed into the street. He was a short, rotund man, and he looked like an angry bulldog as he bustled up to Bull Morgan in the El Dorado and snapped:

"Forty-four of my hosses were run off last night!"

Bull looked down at the irate man for a moment and then hastened to appease him.

"Judge, it wasn't done by anyone that I know. They wouldn't dare."

"I want them back!"

Bull drew the judge aside and talked with him for a while. Gradually the judge became conciliated, and his anger left him.

"Course I should have known better than to think you had a hand in it," he admitted.

"I ain't crazy!" Bull laughed. "An' I'll promise my men will get them back from whoever took them."

168

With that the judge departed, and Bull was left with the unpleasant thought that perhaps some of the men who called him "Boss" had taken them. If that were so, then it would cost him time and money to have them returned.

He was biting savagely at his cigar when Spike Sullivan dismounted before the El Dorado. Spike sauntered in, and after giving Bull a signal to follow him, passed into the back room, which was always deserted at that time in the morning.

"Boss, Allen started after the gents who took the judge's hosses," Spike whispered.

"I hope he catches 'em!" Bull growled vindictively.

"An' he took seven of the United Stage guards with him. That leaves nearly a hundred of the United Stage's pure-blood hosses with only three men guarding them. Hines didn't want to let his men go, but Allen was stubborn. I was in Fenton and Bill Goar, the gent you planted with the United, hears the whole thing. He says Hines was mad as hops, but Allen was stubborn and makes seven of the best of the United fighting men go with him."

Bull ordered brusquely:

"Spike, you get somethin' to eat. Three drinks — no more. Then fork your horse an' hit for the Wood River where she runs into the Grey Bull. You'll find Shorty Stone an' Bum Rogers thereabouts. You tell 'em to collect a few of the boys an' hit that herd tonight. After you seen them, you head back to Fenton. An' if Allen comes back, or things don't look right, you warn the boys off. Savvy?"

169

"You bet you!"

Well pleased with himself, Spike rattled his spurs and went over to the Chinese restaurant. The task he had just been handed of riding thirty miles before sundown did nothing to deter his pleasure in the fact that he was to have a hand in the humbling of Jack Allen.

Close to twelve that night a tired rider clumped into the El Dorado and whispered to Bull that the raid had been a success. Shorty Jones and Bum Rogers had collected the whole herd, and were headed towards Jackson's Hole with a flying start.

"Gents!" Bull raised his stentorian voice and shouted so that he was heard above the uproar: "Gents, until further notice, the drinks are on the house. Get busy!"

CHAPTER
TWENTY

The Trap

Jim Allen withdrew his eyes from the embers of a small fire into which he had been staring in utter silence for nearly an hour and spoke to his companion:

"It's nearly eleven. Reckon you'd better wake the boys."

Burt Hills rose, stretched cramped muscles, then went to several shadowy forms on the farther side of the fire and commenced to shake the sleeping men.

"Come on! Get up!" he ordered roughly.

Suddenly Allen leaped to his feet and stamped out the fire. "They're comin' this way!"

The men strained their ears and listened. Beneath the heavy timber where they stood on the side of Hook Mountain, was complete darkness. They listened but heard no sound. Ten minutes later they all heard the pounding of many hoofs, which for a time grew nearer and then began to recede in the distance.

"They are heading for Jackson's Hole all right," Hills remarked to Allen.

"Thought they would. But I figgered they *might* take the south fork and head for the Owl Creek Mountains, so I blocked it up here."

171

"Why not stop 'em down at the fork?" Hills asked curiously.

"Night fightin's too risky," Allen explained. "Don't want to lose a single hoss, an' I wants all ten of them men. If I gets 'em, Bull will be plumb discouraged!"

Allen turned to the other men.

"Now, boys, get some brush."

Under his direction the men piled a great pile of brittle branches on the bare slope of the mountains. Allen touched a match to it, and the flame swept up into the sky.

Then far across the hills another tiny flame appeared. It grew larger, then vanished.

"All right, Dutchy is watchin'!" Allen spoke with satisfaction.

At Allen's order, the men swung on their horses and followed him down the trail to the fork, and then in pursuit of the band of horses along the north trail.

They had reached the mouth of the pass when the dawn came. The east was aglow, the sun blazed over the rim of the Big Horn Mountains, and the tracks of the stolen horses lay plain on the trail beneath their feet.

A few miles farther on they commenced to climb. The walls closed in and towered above them. They had just topped a sharp rise when the echoes of a volley of rifle shots rumbled through the pass.

"Dutchy has 'em stopped!" Allen said cheerfully. "Spread out, boys, an' don't let none of them get by you!"

The horse thieves never had a chance to put up a fight. Caught by surprise in the first volley of Dutchy

172

and his brothers, which killed three of them, the rest turned and fled straight into the arms of Allen's men. After their leaders had been knocked from the saddle, the rest threw up their arms and quickly surrendered.

While Allen and his men were busily engaged in disarming and trussing up their seven prisoners, Dutchy and his brothers rounded up the stolen horses and then headed them back down the pass to water and grass. And, curiously enough, when Dutchy joined Allen and the United Stage men at the mouth of the pass, the herd of horses had been increased by nearly fifty head.

"Huh!" one of the United riders cried in surprise. "That's funny. I didn't see none of the judge's horses up there at fust."

"Me neither!" another grinned. "It's sure funny. But I reckon the joke's on Bull Morgan."

The other nodded sadly.

"An' it's too darn good to talk about."

That same day, about six o'clock in the afternoon, a strange procession paraded down the long street of Basin. First came a hundred and fifty horses, then seven bound men and after them three bodies tied to the saddles of as many horses.

All the inhabitants of the small town rushed out to see the strange parade. But Allen marched his prisoners directly to the jail and turned them over to the waiting Toothpick. The United riders herded the one hundred and fifty horses down the street to their corrals at the other end of town.

173

Jim Allen had not finished his explanation to Toothpick before the irate judge arrived to congratulate him.

"Damn the man!" the judge cried. "Bull swore to me his men were not guilty. An' he was laughin' at me all the time. I'm goin' to see that every one of them men is hung up as warnin' to other horse thieves. How did you manage to catch 'em?"

"We trailed 'em an' sorta took 'em by surprise," Allen answered vaguely.

Scarcely had the judge left when another visitor arrived. But this time it was not a friendly one.

"If you're not scared," Johnson said coldly, "you will —"

Toothpick interrupted: "How about puttin' him in jail to join his friends?"

"Shut up, Toothpick," Allen said wearily. "Johnson, you've been talkin' loud. In half an hour I'll leave the United office. You start from the El Dorado. An' I won't be wearin' no star!"

Johnson's eyes gleamed with satisfaction; then he nodded and left the jail for the El Dorado. A few minutes afterward, Allen went the opposite direction to the United offices, where he found the delighted Hines awaiting him.

"I want to talk to you," Allen said. "Bull will sure know you helped me trick him an' he'll be fightin' mad. So you want to watch yourself for a couple of days."

Hines shrugged.

"He wouldn't dare touch me. But you're different."

174

"I'm used to that," Allen answered wearily. "You watch yourself. I got a date now." He moved away, but not yet was he free to keep his appointment with Johnson. As he stepped from the door of the United offices, a little round woman bustled up to him.

"Tell me why you refused to come to supper at my house the other night?" she asked. "I'm Mrs. Chuck Newson."

"I know," Allen said vaguely as his eyes searched the street for Johnson.

"Then you'll come tonight?" she insisted.

"Ma'am, I — I —" he stammered.

The woman stared at his embarrassed face. She noted the pug nose, the queer, setter-like eyes, and the lovable, broad grin.

"Ma'am," he said softly, "I'd sure love to come, but I — I ain't fit."

The woman noticed the sadness in his eyes and sensed his utter loneliness. She had it on her lips to urge him further, but she had no opportunity, for just then he turned his face to her again, and she grew cold at the change. He looked older and his setter eyes had changed to the flaring ones of a wolf.

"Ma'am, you go in there an' stay for five minutes," Allen ordered, and to the woman's own surprise, she obeyed him.

Allen turned and walked slowly forward to meet Johnson. The news of the duel had spread, and every doorway had its spectators. Allen walked slowly forward.

"He don't seem over-eager," someone remarked.

Johnson marked Allen's slow progress with inward satisfaction. As they neared each other he, too, slowed his steps. The two were within twenty feet of each other, and the onlookers waited tensely. Then Johnson's hand flashed to his gun. Came a double roar and the gambler fell sideways on to the jail steps.

"All right, Toothpick," Allen called. "Pull him in."

Grinning broadly, Toothpick lifted Johnson and carried him into the jail. The spectators howled their mirth.

"Darned if the little runt didn't time his steps so Johnson would fall into jail."

Kansas Jones and Spike Sullivan had been interested spectators of this little shooting scrap. For if Johnson had won, their own affair would have been put off until later. As it was, they prepared for what they had to do that night.

Allen was eating his breakfast the following morning when a United teamster hammered on the door and excitedly told him Hines had been laid out during the night. Curious, gaping men were milling about the offices when Allen hurried up. He sent them away and was relieved to find that only a few had entered the room where the crime had been committed.

Allen found the doctor busily attending the badly wounded man. Hines had been found that morning in his office near the open safe, which had been rifled and the papers strewn about the office floor. He had not yet regained consciousness.

Boomer pushed his way into the office and spoke lugubriously:

"This is terrible! Is he dead?"

"Nope. An' he'll live to see the gents what did it hang!"

"That's fine!" Boomer licked dry lips. Although he had nothing to do with the attempted murder, he suspected who was behind it and feared that he would be implicated if the guilty man were exposed. "Looks as if he surprised robbers goin' through his safe."

Allen turned without answering and left the offices. He circled the barns and picked up the trail of two horses which had been tied to some bushes in a creek bottom. Returning to the corral to saddle Princess, he saw Boomer ride out of town.

"I'm plumb curious to see if he goes to the same place certain tracks lead to."

Later that morning an exhausted, breathless Boomer galloped up to Bull Morgan's ranch on the Grey Bull River.

"Bull," he gasped, "Hines ain't dead, and Allen is out picking up your men's trail!"

Bull's face never changed. But presently when Boomer told him of Johnson's failure and of Allen's return with the horses and of how the judge's stock were mixed with the United, Bull's rage knew no bounds.

"The judge's sore, an' he says he's goin' to hang 'em all," Boomer said tonelessly.

"Shut up!" Then Bull turned and shouted some orders. Within five minutes he, Boomer, and three of Bull's best gunmen were headed towards Basin. They had reached Pebble Creek when they met Spike Sullivan and Kansas Jones.

"You fools!" Bull stormed. "You've botched things. Hines ain't dead."

"Well, he's due to be sick for a long time, so what's the difference?" Kansas asked indifferently.

Spike Sullivan spoke up:

"That Allen is sure a bloodhound. We see him trailin' us. He was way back of us, so we rides on hard pan an' back-tracks, but he sticks."

"How come he got so close to you?"

"We stopped an' made camp an' went to sleep. You told us not to show up at your place for a coupla days until the thing sorta blew over."

"An' is he followin' you now?" Bull snapped.

"Naw," Spike answered; "we lost him down where the creek forks."

"Boomer!" Bull cried after a moment's thought. "You back-track along Spike's an' Kansas's trail. Maybe Allen is still huntin' around down there. If he is, you take him south of the sand hills an' bring him up to Dry Creek Ravine. We'll be waitin' for him!"

Boomer paled.

"You're a committee man. An' you do as I say, 'cause, if they ever hang me, they'll put a rope around your neck too. Make up a story. Tell him you found a dead man — anything you want. But bring him. Now get!"

Jim had easily followed the gunmen's trail for the first ten miles. Then he had more difficulty. But, trained as

178

he was from infancy to follow a trail or go hungry, it would have taken an Indian to elude him. On arriving at the forked creeks, Allen studied the marks on the farther side and grinned.

"They sure thinks I'm plumb foolish. One gent goes across the creek up to hard pan, then back to the creek again. But I bet they both went upstream. Just the same I figgers that maybe they is watchin', so I'll pretend they fooled me."

He crossed the creek, kept straight on until over the hill, then circled to the left and struck the creek again. Here he picked up their trail and cautiously followed them. A few miles farther on he left his grey in a hollow, climbed the nearest sand hill and surveyed the broken country with his glasses. He quickly spotted Boomer and the others, who were a scant mile away. After a time he saw two detach themselves and gallop back along the creek.

"Spike and Boomer!" he muttered. "I'm havin' a look at Spike's hoss's tracks."

After the two had passed, Allen went leisurely to the creek until he came across Spike's and Boomer's tracks. Stooping, he examined them.

"Yep, one is the same I been trailin' all mornin'. That cooks your goose, Mr. Spike."

Then he returned to his look-out and watched Bull and Kansas and Bull's three riders through his glasses. An hour later Spike returned and the others hurriedly swung on their horses and galloped towards the sand hills. Allen leisurely followed them.

179

Then topping a high hill, he unslung his glasses and studied the country. He could see no sign of Bull or the others, but a second later he sighted Boomer and another rider just as they dipped into a dry wash. Allen's face paled with a vindictive, maddened fury; then he spoke to Princess and charged furiously into the heart of the sand hills.

CHAPTER
TWENTY-ONE

Jack Allen

A few hours after Jim Allen had started out after the attackers of Hines, Toothpick fed his prisoners and cheered them up by solemnly assuring them the judge was going to have them all hanged in order to make room for the new crop of prisoners to be brought in by Sheriff Allen. Then, well pleased with himself, he jingled his keys, clumped back to the office and prepared to enjoy his noon meal while he awaited Allen's return.

He had poured himself a cup of coffee and cut a huge slice from a juicy steak when an authoritative hammering sent him grumbling to the front door. After a hasty glance through the grill he slid back the bolts and threw the door open.

"How come you're back so soon?" he asked carelessly and turned back to his interrupted meal. But when a few seconds later, with his mouth full of steak, he looked up at the little figure who stood staring at him grimly, Toothpick intuitively sensed a vague difference in the man before him.

The heavily whiskered face, the clothes, the two low-hung guns were the same. Yet Toothpick knew the

181

man was not Jim Allen. When the answer to the riddle forced itself on him, he had a sensation as if someone had poured a bucket of water down his back. This man who stood before Toothpick was Jack-twin Allen and he was in a furious rage.

"You're Toothpick Jarrick." This was a statement and not a question. "Where's Jim?"

The tall, lanky cow-puncher gulped down a huge mouthful and stuttered:

"He went to ketch the gents who murdered Hines."

Then Jack Allen began firing questions at the bewildered and harassed Toothpick who attempted to evade direct answers. But when he found out that Jack Allen already knew most of what had happened in the past two weeks, Toothpick answered freely and even related in detail how Jim had the judge's horses run off in order to turn the mouthpiece of the law against Bull.

"Jim turns thief in order to catch a horse thief," Jack Allen commented coldly.

"But the judge was turnin' gents loose as fast as Jim ketched them," Toothpick hastened to explain.

Jack Allen's face remained hard and showed no sign of his inner feelings, yet if Toothpick had only known it, he had gained a friend by his defence of Jim. Toothpick glared with disgust at Allen for a moment and then continued:

"Jim's been doin' things like he figgered you'd do 'em: arresting folks, runnin' other gents out of town, an' suchlike. But he don't accept no social engagements 'cause he says 'twouldn't be square on the womenfolks."

"Why?"

" 'Cause he says, why it don't make no difference to a gent who is run into the hoosegow if the hombre what runs him in ain't respectable. But it ain't fair to decent ladies to accept things from them under false pretences. An' he says, if they knew he was The Wolf, they'd lock up their houses an' not offer him no more pie."

"So he don't eat pie? An' he sure loves it plenty!" Allen said. "Jim's gone trailin' the gents who attacked Hines?"

"Yeh!"

"Then I figgers, if I trails him, it's the quickest way to meet him!"

An hour later Jack Allen was following the trail taken across the rolling prairie earlier that morning by Jim Allen. Above him the sun shone in a cloudless sky and far off to the north, the west, and the east the serried peaks rose layer on layer.

Little by little Jack Allen's anger died. For he realised that what Jim had done had been for love of him. And Jim Allen was one who never counted the consequences. Hearing that people were betting that Jack Allen dared not come to Basin, it was natural for him to do what he had done without a thought of the morrow. Jim would never stop to think that, if the imposture were discovered, Jack Allen's reputation would have been ruined forever: that people would firmly believe Jack Allen had not dared to come to Basin and had sent his outlawed brother in his place.

"An' if the darned little runt got hisself killed makin' believe he was me, I'd have had to stay dead or cut off

183

my whiskers and gone in for bein' an outlaw down South."

As he neared the place where the creeks forked, Boomer rode from a bunch of poplars and headed directly towards him.

"Howdy, Jack," Boomer cried genially.

"Howdy," Jack returned, then commented to himself: "He sure knows me, an' I wish I knew who he was. That darned little Jim has sure got me in a mess."

"You trailin' the gents that downed Hines?" Boomer asked.

"Yeh, I knows who they is, an' I'm goin' now to collect 'em."

Boomer's eyes flickered, and he shifted uneasily in his saddle. None of this was lost on Jack Allen, and a suspicion leaped to his mind that the man before him was not a friend.

Boomer cried with a forced hilarity:

"It was sure a lucky day for this country when I made my colleagues let me write to you an' ask you to come up to the Big Horn country."

So this was the man who had written. Then he must be Amos Boomer. Allen breathed easier, and his suspicions of the moment before died a natural death. For the man who was instrumental in sending for him must perforce be a friend.

"I was on my way to fetch you," Boomer said. Then hesitating for a moment, he added: "I got another dead man to show you. I stumbled on his body in Dry Creek. Shot from behind. He's a rancher named Smith, and I figgered you'd want to look around while the trail was fresh."

"How far is Dry Creek?" Jack Allen asked.

"About six miles. I'll show you."

Allen nodded, and the two turned their horses and headed towards the sand hills. Allen diligently encouraged Boomer to talk and directed the conversation to the events of the past few weeks, for he wished to learn as many details of Jim's activities as possible.

He was determined that the imposture must never be discovered. Jim would have to return to that desolate home of his in the Painted Desert while he, Jack, finished the work of cleaning up the horse thieves.

Boomer talked freely until they entered the waste sand hills. Then he became silent and seemed visibly to shrink and become smaller as his nervousness grew. He recalled all the tales he had heard of Jack Allen and became uneasy and afraid. He shivered and mopped his glistening red face as he thought of what the consequences would be if Jack Allen were to discover his treachery. There would be no more blue skies for him.

"This is Dry Creek," Boomer exclaimed as he turned into a ravine, a dried watercourse, with steep, crumbling banks.

It was crooked — nearly as crooked as the man who thought he was leading Jack Allen to his death. They followed a little, faint animal trail that wound among giant boulders and lonely clumps of sagebrush along the bottom of the arroyo.

"The dead gent is at the farther end."

185

Jack Allen nodded, and Boomer sighed with relief as his keen glance detected no suspicion on the other's face. If he had allowed the matter to rest there, Allen would have been shot from his saddle and died without knowing what hit him. But instead he added:

"This here's a short cut to my place, and that's how I come to find the corpse."

"Short cut —" Allen questioned himself, and his suspicions leaped to life again.

If Boomer had travelled that way that morning, where were his tracks? The trail was free from all signs. No one had come by since the rains of the week before. Then Boomer lied.

Having arrived at that conclusion, Allen acted with the speed and precision that were characteristic of his brother Jim. He instinctively knew he was in a trap, and he whirled his pony behind Boomer's. As he did so, three rifles cracked ahead of him, and the slugs whistled viciously close.

His first instinct was to make a run back the way he had come, but he intuitively realised that the trap had closed behind him there. So he drove his horse into a headlong gallop and headed for a wide break in the ravine's walls. And as he went, rifles spat their leaden slugs after him.

He dashed through the opening of the ravine and found himself hemmed in by the high, sheer walls of a former tributary of Dry Creek. To go back was impossible, so he drove his horse forward. Behind him came the drumming of hard-ridden horses. A moment's thought convinced him that this was no

186

place to make a stand. If he stopped, his enemies would have him at their mercy.

The bed of the old creek became so rough that Allen was forced to slow down his headlong pace. He picked his way between the naked boulders for another two hundred yards, when he saw that the creek bed ended and the way was blocked by a rocky cliff. If he could not find a way out of that, he was trapped. Then his horse, which had been hit by the first volley of bullets, staggered, slid to his knees, rolled over, and lay still.

Badly shaken by the fall, Allen thought his leg had been broken again. But when he regained his feet he found that, although the pain was severe, he could still hobble. He tried to pull out his rifle which was jammed in its sheath beneath the dead horse. Then a bullet splintered on a rock before him and filled his face with dust. Another whined close to his ears. He still tugged at his rifle, for his one chance of life lay in getting it free.

Then another volley of shots forced him to abandon his efforts and duck towards a pile of rocks close under the bank of the ravine. For the moment he was safe there. But he knew he was trapped and doomed to death, bar some miracle as yet unforeseen. His enemies had only to climb the banks of the ravine, and they would have him at their mercy.

There was just a chance they thought he had a rifle, and that would delay their attack. But even with the delay, there was little Jack Allen could do.

A big, burly man climbed a rock a scant hundred yards down the ravine and leisurely commenced to direct the movement of his men. Then Jack Allen knew that they realised he was armed only with a pistol. His only chance lay in Jim's coming.

Jack knew from Toothpick that his outlaw brother had set out in pursuit of the attackers of Hines, and these men, Jack was certain, had been the tools of the committee man. His only chance was that Jim should trail them in time.

Five minutes later Jack Allen saw a man slowly crawl up the farther end of the ravine. He was fully two hundred yards away, and it was impossible for Jack to score a hit at that distance. Foot by foot the man made his slow way up the steep wall of the ravine. He had just thrust his hand over the top, and Jack Allen was gathering himself for a hopeless dash for his rifle when the drumming of a fast-ridden horse made him hesitate.

The climber paused, drew himself to the top, glanced over, then with an oath slid hastily down the slant walls. Allen heard him shout an unintelligible something to Bull who vanished from his perch on the rock.

The drumming hoofs drew nearer and nearer, then ceased. From the rim of the arroyo there came the savage cry of the fiercest, most ruthless and bravest of all wild things. The cry of the grey wolf as it is about to make a kill!

Jack Allen's tense face broke into a triumphant grin; then he shouted exultantly:

"The trappers is trapped!"

Lifting up his voice, he gave forth an answering call — the battle cry of the Allens — the barking snarl of the desert wolf!

188

CHAPTER
TWENTY-TWO

Honey Boy Goes

It was Spike Sullivan whom Jack Allen had watched laboriously climb to the rim of the arroyo and then slide precipitately down again. Spike's face was white and scared as he picked himself up and bellowed to Bull Morgan:

"Jack Allen's up there!"

Bull hastily descended from his perch on the tall rock and advanced on the quaking Spike.

"What you talkin' about? We got Jack Allen holed up over there."

Spike's eyes dropped before the irate gaze of his boss. He glanced dubiously along the rim of the ravine and said sullenly:

"If it ain't him, it's his ghost. I seen him, whiskers an' all, burnin' the ground on that grey of his'n!"

It was then that the call of the grey wolf made them all glance wonderingly to the rim of the ravine. And when Jack's answering call came, even Bull moved uneasily. There was something so savage, so relentless in that call, that for a moment every man there was thrown off his balance, as if suddenly confronted by something entirely beyond comprehension.

Kansas Jones paled visibly beneath his tan, glanced nervously towards the rim, and muttered:

"If I was down along the border, I'd sure believe the Killer Wolf was up there!"

"The Killer Wolf?" Boomer questioned.

"Jim-twin Allen, the outlaw. Twin brother to the gent we thought we had cornered over there. An' I'm tellin' you, if The Wolf is up along that rim, we can one an' all kiss ourselves good-bye!"

With that, Kansas turned and walked briskly to where he had left his horse. Bull knew that he was hopelessly committed to this adventure and that, if he allowed Kansas to desert, the others would follow. So he yanked out his gun and asked coldly:

"Where you goin'?"

"Me? I'm hittin' the breeze. I ain't fightin' no Wolf," Kansas answered without turning.

Bull snapped decisively:

"You're helpin' me plant Jack Allen, or I'm droppin' you. If we don't get Allen's scalp, we'll all swing 'cause he knows we all had a hand in cashin' Hines!"

Kansas paused. After a moment he nodded.

"That wolf's call sorta took my nerve. But you're sure right, boss. We got to down Jack Allen, or we all gets strangled!"

"I had nothin' to do with it!" Boomer protested frantically. He looked half his usual size — like a partly deflated balloon. What little courage he had had disappeared before the fear of the noose.

Bull glanced contemptuously at him.

190

"Spike," he said, "you take one man and go up an' help cash Jack Allen. Kansas, you, me, an' the others spread out. Keep covered and watch the rim!"

Followed by a thin, scrawny man, Spike slipped cautiously towards the two riders who were watching Jack Allen. The others scattered and dodged behind cover and peered upwards to the rim. Kansas saw a tuft of grass move and instantly fired at it. A taunting, happy laugh came floating down in answer to his shot.

"That's sure enough The Wolf!" Kansas cried with an oath. Then cautiously he began to make his way down the ravine towards the horses.

"You boys spread out," Spike ordered when he reached the locality where Jack Allen crouched behind his cover. "I'm goin' to circle behind them rocks an' take him from t'other side."

The others watched Spike crawl from rock to rock until he had obtained a position on the farther side of Jack Allen. He peered from behind a clump of sagebrush and brought his rifle to his shoulder. As he did so, a rifle cracked from the rim and Spike sprang to his feet, took a few wavering steps, and pitched forward on his face.

Instantly every eye switched to the rim. Then a cool voice floated down to them.

"I'm talkin' to the ugly gent with the red handkerchief. I don't like his hat!"

Came the crack of a rifle and the hat of the man who wore the red handkerchief flew from his head. The man clutched his shoulder and screamed:

"I quits! I give up!"

191

The two remaining riders hastily wormed their way back towards Bull who was crawling forward to learn the result of the firing.

"Spike's dead, an' Bill has his arm broke. We can't do nothin'. We can't spot the gent up there. He keeps shiftin' his place an' firin' through the grass along the rim."

"We got to get farther down the arroyo to where it spreads out," Bull said, after a moment's thought. He crawled forward to Boomer and confided: "I'm goin' to take one man with me an' try to work down to where we can get up to the rim."

Boomer wiped his dry lips and nodded. Then he burrowed into the sand that protected him from being seen by the man on the rim.

"That yellow-bellied Kansas is aimin' to make a run for it!" Bull stormed. Angered at this treachery, Bull raised his rifle to his shoulder.

Kansas had decided that the man on the rim, even if he were not the border wolf, was more to be feared than Bull. So he had made his way to where the horses were and hastily flung himself into the saddle. But hardly had the horse moved away from the others when Bull's rifle spat, and Kansas swayed and tumbled to the ground.

A voice came from the rim.

"Boomer, I see you behind that big black rock. I ain't cashin' you in, 'cause I want to save you to have your neck stretched. But if you don't stand up quick with your hands up, I shoot!"

Boomer burrowed deeper into the sand.

"You got three more seconds, Boomer!"

At that, Boomer sprang upright and held his hands above his head.

"Let your gun drop. Go out in the middle of that sand spot and lie down on your face," the voice commanded.

With trembling fingers, Boomer obeyed.

"Now the gent behind that split rock foller suit!" the voice commanded a moment later. "You got big pearl buttons on your shirt, an' I can see you plain."

The man made a dive from his position and flung himself behind a slanting rock which completely concealed him from the rim. But he had hardly finished congratulating himself when a voice directly behind him snapped:

"Do as you're told or I'll drill you!"

Jack Allen had slowly crept forward along the farther side of the ravine and was now directly behind the man who, caught between two fires, followed the example of Boomer and lay down beside him. A moment later another man was caught in an exposed position and forced to join the other two.

In the meanwhile, Bull and the last rider were scrambling down the ravine towards the horses. Jim Allen could move twice as fast along the rim as they, and he reached a position opposite the horses and waited for them to appear. A few seconds later they crawled from behind some loose rock, and Allen dropped a shot directly before Bull which filled the rustler's eyes with sand and his mouth with helpless blasphemy.

"Cave, Bull, or I'll cash you!" Jim Allen commanded.

Bull glanced up and noted the rifle which covered him from the rim. He slowly arose to his feet, dropped his belt to the ground, and raised his hands above his head. His companion hastened to follow his example, and the two obeyed orders and went up the ravine where they lay down beside the others.

Allen called his grey, sprang into the saddle, and rode down the ravine a short distance to where the banks shelved. Here he slid to the bottom. Then picking his way along the floor to where the seven horses were tied, he collected the ropes from the saddles and made his way to where the five men were lying. They had heard him ride away, and Bull had raised his head sharply. But after receiving a warning from Jack Allen he lay down quietly.

Jim bound the prisoners' hands and arms together quickly and skilfully; then he ordered them to their feet and herded them to the waiting horses. When they had moved away he turned to Jack and said softly:

"Them gents ain't never seen us together, so they don't savvy they is two of us. I'm takin' 'em to jail 'cause you ain't fit. You wait until dark and slide into town inconspicuous-like. I'll leave Kansas's horse for you. He won't be needin' it." He paused for a moment and then said with a grimace: "You can raise your hell then; I'll be waitin' for you!"

"I'm sure goin' to give you a drubbin'!" Jack swore fondly as Jim moved off after the prisoners.

Just as the long, slanting rays of the sun struck the piles of bottles and made them gleam diamondwise, as they had the first time Jim Allen entered Basin, so they did now at his last entrance.

Once more the streets of Basin offered a way for a strange procession. The loafers stared; then rushed into the saloons where they shrieked their news.

"Jack Allen has got Bull Morgan and Boomer tied up like chickens and is takin' 'em to jail."

From the houses, the saloons, the hotels and stores, the entire population poured into the street. Everyone gaped and stared at the five men who, in single file, moved towards the jail. Each was bound, and from the neck of each one there ran a rope to the next. Behind them, one horse carried the dangling bodies of Spike Sullivan and Kansas Jones.

And a small, grim-faced man brought up the rear. He rode jauntily erect, with one hand stroking his beard and the other hovering over the butt of a Colt. People whispered and shouted. Some swore; some jeered as they pointed to the sullen-faced Bull and the trembling, terror-stricken Boomer. It was a triumph — a conqueror returning with his prisoners; such a procession as Rome had seen on a larger scale many centuries before.

Friends of Bull stamped about, whispered, and made hasty plans for a rescue. But they lacked a leader and each one feared to make a play that might go unbacked by his friends. Before the plans had crystallised, the procession had halted before the jail, and the prisoners were being lifted from their horses without ceremony and hustled within doors.

While Toothpick was roughly urging the prisoners through the jail door, Jim Allen sat on his grey with a

195

gun in each hand and held back both the curious and the friends of Bull.

"I'm tellin' you, gents!" he warned. "Some of you is friendly, but I'm tellin' you that the first one what crowds me, I'm considerin' his intentions hostile an' will drop him!"

"How comes Kansas an' t'other got beefed?" someone asked when the last of the prisoners had vanished within the jail.

"Him? He's Bull's partner. They tries to kill Hines 'cause they wants to appoint another committee man what is friendly with Boomer. Then they has a majority an' can run things to suit themselves. Then they fires me and has Kansas Jones made sheriff," Allen explained.

"How comes Kansas an' t'other got beefed?" someone else asked, and pointed to the two dangling figures.

"Them? I follows the two gents what attacks Hines clear up to Bull's place. Bull and Boomer figgers I know too much, so they try to bushwhack me, and in the ruckus what follows, Kansas an' t'other one cashes."

"Who was with you?"

For a second Allen hesitated, then said:

"No one. I was alone."

With that Allen swung down from Princess and entered the jail. After he had vanished the men looked at each other with curious eyes.

"He was alone. One against seven!"

"He's a hellion!"

"He ain't tol' it all. I'd sure like to seen that scrap, an' I'm aimin' to learn about it."

But neither the speaker nor anyone else was ever to learn the truth. For although the prisoners knew that Allen had a friend with him they never saw him and could not identify him. The only man who could have told was Kansas Jones, and his lips would never speak.

It was much later that night when the two brothers ate their dinner in the jail office. Jim Allen had shaved his face and was dressed in his old tattered clothes. They ate in silence. When the meal was finished, Jim looked up and said with his broad, cheerful grin:

"When you givin' me this drubbin'?"

"When I next sees you," Jack replied gruffly.

They were silent for a moment. Each loved the other more than anything in the world. Each in a way was set aside from his neighbours. For a gunman, a killer, could have no friends. Fear does not go hand in hand with friendship; both were lonely; and both knew, when they separated, it would be long odds if ever they would see each other again.

Mrs. Newson had sent over a pie made from the apples sent to her from Vermont. But Jim pushed his piece away and said heavily:

"Reckon I'd better drift!"

"Guess so."

"That grey of yours, Honey Boy, is a right fine hoss. I learned him to eat pie an' talk," Jim spoke cheerfully as they went round to the back of the jail where Toothpick was holding the saddled Princess.

"It sure seems funny to only have one hoss," Jim confided as he swung into the saddle. Jack Allen looked up at his brother with a smile at once quizzical and fond.

"Take the hoss," he said. "He's yours."

Jim Allen grinned sheepishly.

"So-long!"

"So-long," the two on the ground replied.

They stood there until Jim-twin Allen had vanished in the darkness. As they rounded the corner of the jail, the night was split by a shrill, uncanny whistle. From the corral in the rear came the answering neigh of a horse, a splintering crash and pounding hoofs down the road.

"Reckon that was Honey Boy," Toothpick chuckled. "Jim sure learned him to answer that whistle."

"The darned little rascal!" Jack Allen growled. "I sure will give him a drubbin' when I sees him next year!"

Harold 'Hal' C. Dunning came from Westport, Connecticut, resided there most of his life, and is buried in the Dunning family plot in the Episcopal Cemetery in Cedarhurst. He was a short story writer for Street & Smith magazines for most of his life. Like Clarence E. Mulford, who created Hopalong Cassidy, Dunning wrote Western fiction while living primarily in the eastern United States. Unlike Mulford who maintained a permanent residence, Dunning was a creature of hotel rooms—even after he married—and eschewed permanent residence anywhere, living in a hotel in Quebec, Canada, with his family in Westport, and hotels in Flushing, New York; Newport, Rhode Island; Provincetown, Massachusetts, and in Westport. He was visiting a friend in Greenwich Village, New York when he died of a heart attack on July 29, 1931. What supported this itinerant lifestyle was the tremendous popularity of his character known as the White Wolf, outlaw Jim-twin Allen whose eyes were flecked with yellow and wolf-slanted. He rode alone with his two gray cow ponies, Princess and Gray Combat. The one man Jim-twin Allen could trust was his brother, Sheriff Jack-twin Allen, and often the little, freckle-faced gunman would come to his aid. The White Wolf stories were showcased in Street & Smith's *Complete Stories*, a bi-weekly supported largely by Hal Dunning's stories. Several of these stories were welded together to form books, all, published by Chelsea House: *The Outlaw Sheriff* (1928), *White Wolf's Law* (1928), *White Wolf's Pack* (1929), *The Wolf Deputy* (1930), *White Wolf's Feud* (1930), and the posthumous *White Wolf's Outlaw Legion* (1933). When Dunning died so unexpectedly, Street & Smith was faced with a financial crisis since *Complete Stories* could not survive without Jim-twin Allen. Author Frederick C. Davis was hired to continue the stories under the Hal Dunning byline, while Mrs. Cecily Dunning, the author's widow, was paid $60 every time her husband's name was used. Toward the end of the decade the Jim-twin Allen stories were continued by Walker A. Tompkins writing as Hal Dunning in Street & Smith's *Wild West Weekly*.

Gloucester
Tube

118   Cromwell RD
              LnD
        SW 7 4 T